"What do  Ranger?"

"I'm on a leave to his boot cas my leg."

Which told Eden nothing.

"So," Rio said, "what else do you do here with the veterans?"

"We talk and I listen. Most have regular doctor's visits and prefer to go with one of us."

"Why's that?"

"Why do you think?" She gave his shoulder a bump. "We're more fun!"

He smirked. "Muffins? Santa hats? Dancing reindeer?"

Seeing the humor in his eyes, she batted her lashes at him. "When the occasion warrants."

"What do you do when it's no longer the holidays?"

"There is always something to celebrate."

"Yeah?"

Eden widened her eyes at him. "Yeah."

Was she flirting with the guy? Was he flirting with her? Did she want him to?

"Come on. Wes, in Room 7, was a Ranger, too. He'll want to meet you."

Something flickered in Rio's expression. Enough to make her wonder once again about the secrets hidden behind the cool facade.

Linda Goodnight, a *New York Times* bestselling author and winner of a RITA® Award in Inspirational Fiction, has appeared on the Christian bestseller list. Her novels have been translated into more than a dozen languages. Active in orphan ministry, Linda enjoys writing fiction that carries a message of hope in a sometimes-dark world. She and her husband live in Oklahoma. Visit her website, lindagoodnight.com, for more information.

Books by Linda Goodnight

Love Inspired

House of Hope

Redeeming the Past
Keeping His Promise
His Christmas Journey Home

Sundown Valley

To Protect His Children
Keeping Them Safe
The Cowboy's Journey Home
Her Secret Son
The Rancher's Sanctuary
To Protect His Brother's Baby

The Buchanons

Cowboy Under the Mistletoe
The Christmas Family
Lone Star Dad
Lone Star Bachelor

Love Inspired Trade

Claiming Her Legacy

Visit the Author Profile page at LoveInspired.com for more titles.

HIS CHRISTMAS JOURNEY HOME

LINDA GOODNIGHT

If you purchased this book without a cover you should be aware that this book is stolen property. It was reported as "unsold and destroyed" to the publisher, and neither the author nor the publisher has received any payment for this "stripped book."

ISBN-13: 978-1-335-23016-4

Recycling programs for this product may not exist in your area.

His Christmas Journey Home

Copyright © 2025 by Linda Goodnight

All rights reserved. No part of this book may be used or reproduced in any manner whatsoever without written permission.

Without limiting the author's and publisher's exclusive rights, any unauthorized use of this publication to train generative artificial intelligence (AI) technologies is expressly prohibited.

This is a work of fiction. Names, characters, places and incidents are either the product of the author's imagination or are used fictitiously. Any resemblance to actual persons, living or dead, businesses, companies, events or locales is entirely coincidental.

For questions and comments about the quality of this book, please contact us at CustomerService@Harlequin.com.

® is a trademark of Harlequin Enterprises ULC.

Love Inspired
22 Adelaide St. West, 41st Floor
Toronto, Ontario M5H 4E3, Canada
www.LoveInspired.com

Printed in U.S.A.

Then spake Jesus again unto them, saying,
I am the light of the world: he that followeth me shall
not walk in darkness, but shall have the light of life.
—*John* 8:12

Grief comes to us all, but the accidental death of a healthy toddler is especially excruciating. So, this book is dedicated in memory of my granddaughter, Irina Rose (Rosey Posey), who brought so much light and joy into the world during her short life. We miss her so much, but trust that she is now laughing with Jesus and waiting for us to someday join her. We love you, Baby Girl.

Chapter One

His fingers were cold, numb, losing function.

But what had he expected? Riding a motorcycle cross-country in December may not have been his best idea. After four years in West Africa following another six in the Middle East, his body had acclimated to heat and more heat. Not that Rio Hendrix paid that much attention to his body's needs.

Most of the time.

Except when his fingers stopped working.

Rio pulled the sweet new Harley to a stop below a city limits sign. Powerful engine rumbling beneath him, he flipped up his helmet and removed his gloves to flex his stiff hands as he gazed around the quiet rural landscape.

Southern Oklahoma air was cold this time of year, but nothing like the East Coast freezer he'd left three days ago. Or rather, been booted out of until the investigation was completed. His intelligence op had been breached and he as well as two other operatives were, at the least, compromised and at the worst, guilty.

Rio clenched his jaw, anger rising. If there was

one thing he was, it was loyal, especially to his country. For fifteen years, he'd risked his life in the most dangerous places on the planet to stop the bad actors of this world. He certainly wouldn't breach an important op.

But someone had.

So, a man who rarely requested a day off was forced to take a leave of absence. Indefinitely.

"Don't call us, we'll call you," was the message his handler had delivered.

Arguing was fruitless. The big boys had spoken. Guys in his line of work weren't even acknowledged by Uncle Sam. Understandable. He'd known the rules when he'd been recruited. In his naive youth, he'd found the secrecy and adventure exciting.

His gut gnawed, both with hunger and stress, and he was not the stressing kind of guy. Cool under pressure, unruffled in the most dangerous situations, yet the thought of losing the only life he knew had him toting Tums and gulping Mylanta.

He yanked a pack of antacids from inside his leather jacket and popped a few.

A passing semi left a wake of cold air.

What would he do if he couldn't go back? If Uncle Sam decided he was no longer valuable regardless of how many languages he spoke and how many successful missions he'd completed.

The secret work he did for the US government in enemy territory was all he knew. No family, no outside life. Most people didn't even know Rio

Hendrix existed. Until four days ago, the only close friends he'd ever known hadn't heard from him in ten years. Until he'd telephoned John-Parker Wisdom, they'd thought he was dead. Might be easier if he was.

But Rio had never taken the easy way out. Stop the bad guys. Do the right thing, even when it hurt; a moral code that had landed him in foster care at age twelve.

The burning gut flamed higher.

Wouldn't do to think about *that* situation today.

Sticking both hands under his jacket to warm them, he contemplated a future scarier than being embedded with a terrorist cell for four and a half years. Men who would gleefully torture him to death if they discovered he was stealing their secrets.

Rio rolled his shoulders, stretched his back.

Did he even know how to function in civilized society anymore?

He was about to find out. With nowhere else to go except crazy, Rio had accepted a shocking invitation from his former best pal and foster brother, John-Parker Wisdom. Old JP was getting married.

Rio didn't much believe in Providence, but he wondered how the invitation had managed to find him at the opportune time, a time when he desperately needed to do something with himself besides brood.

Miss Mamie would have called it a God thing.

He still couldn't imagine Mamie's house without her in it. She'd been a good woman, a light in his darkest hours, although the angry, rebellious boy hadn't understood how fortunate he'd been to be placed into a foster home run by Mamie Bezek.

He knew now, when it was too late to tell her, thank her.

Studying the barren winter landscape on the outskirts of town—a dapple of houses surrounded by rolling farmland, cows, horses and long barbed-wire fences—his attention returned to the giant green-and-white city limits sign.

Welcome to Rosemary Ridge. Home of 7,623 Friendly Folks and 5 or 6 Old Cranks.

Rio snorted.

He'd known a few of those old cranks. Rather, they'd known him. Rio, the troublemaker, the smart kid with the bad attitude.

With a twist of his lips, he muttered, "Time to get reacquainted."

Replacing his gloves, Rio flipped down his visor, revved the engine and roared toward the unsuspecting little town.

Walking dogs was not intended to be a blood sport. Eden Carnegie was as certain of this as she was of her love for all things Christmas.

In fact, disaster was the last thing on her mind this cold, sunshiny day. Her thoughts, like the Santa hat on her head and the jingle bells on her dog's bright red collar, were about Christmas. Christmas, veterans, and the dogs she was obedience training for two clients. Extra money that would help pay for this year's annual Celebrate Veterans Christmas Party, of which she was the head honcho, as Grandpa would say.

Ideas for the event swirled in her head as she and the three dogs jaunted along the side street toward downtown. Star, the sheltie client, and Brinkley, Eden's rescued mutt, trotted along at the ends of a triple leash. Lucky, the handsome brindle boxer, led the way, his proud head held high like a king surveying his kingdom. They were nice dogs, but then, Eden had never met a dog she didn't like. Even the ones that required a muzzle. They were scared, not mean, and as a groomer, she met all kinds.

Star and Lucky were doing great in their training and little Brinkley was always well-mannered, so she let her mind wander to Christmas decorations for the big party.

Maybe this year's tree would be flocked white with handmade red-and-blue ornaments bearing each attendee's name and branch of service. A keepsake. Or maybe she'd decorate in a vintage style with bubble lights, paper candles, candy-striped finials and strands of popcorn.

Enthusiasm growing, Eden envisioned stringing popcorn with the vets while they listened to old-fashioned Christmas carols and shared stories of their childhood Christmases.

Strolling the streets of downtown Rosemary Ridge always gave her more ideas. With its highly decorated, hundred-year-old, red-brick buildings, her hometown was as pretty as a Christmas Hallmark movie.

Exposure to people and cars was good training for the dogs, so, at the corner, she'd cross the street, make the turn and head in that direction. Even from this eastern edge of town, the glow of Christmas lights and the double row of small pine trees festooned with red bows positioned in front of stores along Main Street was visible. And festive.

Rosemary Ridge knew how to celebrate holidays and Christmas was the biggest and brightest. Another reason to make Celebrate Veterans even better this year. In Eden's view, everyone, especially veterans living in long-term care without family, should experience a wonder-filled holiday, complete with food and gifts and comradery.

She and her co-volunteers would make that happen. If they could raise enough money.

Because of the struggling economy, money was tight and donations down this year.

Eden pressed her lips together but quickly brightened. Worry was the opposite of faith. And if there was one thing Eden had in abundance, it was faith.

"'All things work together for good to them that love God,'" she quoted to the dogs. "And I do. So that's that."

At the corner, she tugged gently on the triple leash. "Sit."

All three dogs plopped onto their bottoms.

"Good dogs. Good dogs." She patted each head

before returning her attention to downtown and the party.

In fact, the three dogs were behaving so well, she completely lost focus on the job at hand. Only for a moment.

But a moment was all it took for disaster to strike.

It wasn't that she didn't hear the rumble of an engine. She did. Surely, the dogs heard it, too.

The noise grew louder. Much louder.

Suddenly, without warning, Lucky the boxer lunged. The smaller dogs had no choice but to follow. Neither did Eden.

The next few minutes happened in a blur of motion and noise. Barking dogs, a roaring engine.

Heart pounding in her chest, Eden jerked at the leashes tethered to her wrist. A mistake. She knew better. But too late.

The out-of-control dogs lurched in different directions. Brinkley yelped and tried to climb her leg, twisting his leash. Star spun to the right and wrapped around Eden's ankles. Lucky charged into the street. And headed directly toward the oncoming motorcycle.

Eden yanked hard but the boxer yanked harder. Athletic shoes skidding, she was mid-street before she knew it.

She had a quick impression of sunlight glinting off a monstrous black machine and a rider all in black. Like Darth Vader.

The motorcycle loomed nearer, louder, tires screaming.

In a struggle to pull the dogs to safety with her legs entangled, Eden fell. Right in the middle of the street. On top of Lucky.

Three dogs sprawled beneath and around her.

She heard the final, terrifying screech, prayed for mercy and braced for disaster... And then stared in helpless horror as the biker intentionally lay the motorcycle on its side, away from her and the dogs.

The machine slid fifty feet and slammed into the curb.

Shaking, mouth dry as flea powder, Eden, still tangled in the leashes, crawled on all fours toward the accident victim, dragging the yapping dogs with her. A shivering Brinkley, always a coward in tense situations, climbed onto her back.

Though the action made the tangled mess even worse, she tucked her dog beneath her and kept crawling.

Braced against what she might see and murmuring prayers, Eden reached the downed rider.

Pinned beneath the huge Harley, the man yanked off his helmet. Shaggy black tumbled out.

Through gritted teeth, he grunted, "Are you hurt?"

Eden blinked a couple of times to be sure she'd heard correctly.

The guy was concerned about *her* when he was the one lying on the pavement under an enormous, still-rumbling, heat-exuding motorcycle?

Who was this guy?

"I'm fine. What about you?" She unsnapped Brinkley's leash and commanded him to stay in the adjacent grass while she untangled the boxer and the sheltie.

"I'll live." Again, his reply was more grunted than spoken.

From the tension in his very blue eyes and the drawn pale line of his lips, she suspected he was more injured than he wanted her to know.

"Don't move," she told him.

He snorted.

Okay, so that was a dumb thing for her to say. He likely *couldn't* move.

She pointed at him and then the dogs. "I'll be right back."

With only Star and Lucky to deal with, Eden finished untangling their leashes and tethered them to a nearby streetlight. Safe. Out of the way.

She gave Lucky a cranky glare and hurried back to the biker who now attempted, unsuccessfully, to push away the heavy motorcycle. The effort seemed to exhaust him. Sweat beaded his forehead.

So he *was* hurt.

Thank the sweet Lord the biker had skidded to the edge of the street. At least they didn't need to worry about being mowed down by a passing pickup truck.

"Let me help." Eden reached for the handlebars.

"Don't," came the terse reply.

"I'm stronger than I look," she said. "I can do this. Trust me. I'll lift enough for you to slide out."

The pained scowl said he didn't believe her.

Conscience eating her alive, Eden *needed* to help

the poor guy. If not for her, he'd be miles down the road by now.

"I'm a dog groomer. I wrestle large dogs all day and sometimes my grandpa. I can do this."

If he thought the addition of her grandfather was strange, he was too miserable to say so. Grandpa mostly took care of his own needs but occasionally the COPD made him too breathless to maneuver on his own. Eden provided a sturdy shoulder.

"Try first. Show me you can lift." Again, he grunted the words. "Carefully. My Harley's new."

His Harley? What about his trapped leg?

"I'd be insulted at your dubious attitude if this wasn't all my fault."

The man didn't reply. He was too busy gritting his teeth.

He was hurt all right. How badly was the question.

"Here we go." Eden, needing all one hundred and ten pounds of muscle she used on mastiffs and great Danes, raised the motorcycle a few inches. "I can hold it. Let's do this."

"A couple more inches?" He pushed at the seat with leather-gloved hands.

Straining but determined, Eden braced her legs and shoved upward another three inches. This thing was heavy!

Wary, pain-filled dark eyes locked on hers. "Whatever you do, don't turn loose."

"I'm good." *For about another minute or two. Please, Jesus, give me strength.* "Now move, and hurry."

"Can't," he grunted. "My leg's broken."

"Oh." The word came out in a dismayed squeak and she almost weakened. Guilt pierced her.

Seeing the man's gritty determination, she muttered a prayer, "Jesus, help me," locked one knee beneath the heated metal and pushed for all she was worth.

Her arms trembled, but she stayed the course as the man she'd injured gingerly slid his body away from the Harley. The effort had to hurt, but he moved faster than she thought possible with a suspected broken bone.

Just when she thought she'd fold, he cleared the motorcycle and collapsed against the curb. He panted; his chest rose and fell beneath the black leather jacket. Sweat beaded his scowling forehead.

Eden gently lowered the machine and then fell back next to him against the curb, out of breath, too, still trembling. Brinkley whined for permission to join her.

"Come on, Brink." She patted the side of her thigh.

The little black mutt trotted over and licked her cheek. She snuggled him against her hip. He wiggled away to share his licks with the injured man.

In appreciation, the guy stroked Brinkley's scraggly fur and almost smiled.

Brownie points for the biker.

Satisfied he'd done his job, Brinkley offered the man one final nuzzle before returning to Eden's side.

Voices came from across the street.

The biker glanced toward the gathering crowd and back at her. The purest blue eyes she'd ever seen glinted with humor. "They're just in time to be too late."

She had to admire a man who could find the humor at a time like this. And who liked dogs.

"You're hurt, young man." The new arrival was Wink Myrick, an old cowboy whose hat looked bigger than his head. "Better get you to the ER."

Wink's much larger brother Frank, in denim overalls, said, "You all right, little lady?"

"Yes, Mr. Frank, but he's not. I'm about to call 9-1-1." She hoped her phone hadn't suffered in the fall.

As she extracted it from her back jeans' pocket, five powerful, leather-clad fingers clamped on her wrist. "No ambulance."

"But—"

"I got my car 'round the corner," Frank said. "I'll run get it and cart you to the ER."

"No." The biker's tone was terse and final. "I'm not leaving my bike here."

Of all the idiotic statements. "Seriously?"

"It's new."

Eden couldn't help it. She rolled her eyes. Then, being of the frame of mind that courtesy was the better route, she smiled at the older gentleman.

"Thank you, Mr. Frank. This stubborn man refuses an ambulance, but I think he'll change his mind when he realizes he can't walk that far. And I can't carry him."

"He sure looks familiar." Frank leaned in, squinting at the biker as if he didn't have ears to hear. "Wink," he said, "do we know this feller?"

"We must. We know everybody, but I can't think of his name right off." Wink scratched his ear. "Give me a minute and I'll remember."

Eden thought the man looked familiar, too. Long, coal-black hair, mussed from the helmet, flopped forward on his forehead. Blue eyes and alpha-male bone structure gave him a face that probably broke hearts all over the place, but several days' beard and his current frown of pain gave him a slightly sinister appearance.

Having regained her usual energy, Eden pushed to a stand to confer with the Myrick brothers. In the process, she checked on the dogs lying in the brown grass.

The stubborn biker dude fished out his own cell phone and started a conversation with someone.

He squinted up at Eden. "Where are we? What street?"

"Main and Bell."

He repeated the words into the phone and hung up. "My buddy will be here in a minute." To Wink and Frank he said, "Can you fellas help me stand?"

"You can't get up," Eden argued. "Your leg is injured, broken, you said."

"I have a spare one." Again, humor broke through the pain. "Can't have my buddy see me sprawled on the side of the road like a dead possum."

"Man pride." Eden shook her head. She encountered it daily in caring for her grandpa and in the veterans she assisted. As Grandpa reminded her, when a man had nothing else left, let him keep his pride. That was the reason she gave in.

"Wink, Frank, can you stand this stubborn man upright?"

"Sure can. Why, I wrangle steers and heifers three times his weight. Grab hold, Frank."

The biker wasn't small by any means. Hoisting him would take both of the older gentlemen.

As Wink and Frank stood the biker on his one useful leather-booted foot, a huge blue pickup truck squealed to a halt beside them. John-Parker Wisdom, a friend of hers who'd founded the new foster home for teenage boys, hopped out. His business partner, Brandt James, shot out of the passenger side and rounded the vehicle. Eden knew both from high school, although they'd been a couple of years ahead of her. Veterans themselves, they contributed to the Christmas party.

Each nodded toward her and the older gentlemen, but their focus was the one-legged biker.

"You old scoundrel," John-Parker said. "Man, I was surprised to get your phone call."

"Never thought we'd see your ugly mug again," Brandt added, hands on hips, a grin on his face, as if the man in question wasn't standing there on one leg like a flamingo in dire need of medical attention.

"Could we save the happy reunion for later, boys? I got a problem needs dealt with."

John-Parker laughed. "Got yourself in another mess. Some things don't change."

The man jerked his head toward the pickup truck. "Load my Harley first."

"You're blocking traffic. You're going first."

He rested a hand on John-Parker's shoulder. "Not leaving without my bike."

"Shut up," Brandt said amiably. "You called for rescue; we're on the case."

All three grinned as if sharing a joke.

Men. Though she surrounded herself with them, she couldn't say she fully understood them. She did, however, appreciate their muscles.

And clearly, the trio knew each other well.

As Brandt and John-Parker each shoved a shoulder under one of the biker's arms, Eden squinted toward the handsome face again. Memories clinked into place.

Three foster boys, a trio that ran together in high school. Miss Mamie's street rats, they'd called themselves.

Eden recognized the handsome biker now.

Rio Hendrix, school heartthrob and genius bad boy was back in town.

And she, with help from her dogs, had broken the poor man's leg.

Chapter Two

Rio was not a good patient. The ER nurses had wanted to cut the leg of his leather pants and that was not happening. He'd paid five hundred dollars for these babies. After a significant tussle during which he'd threatened to hobble out of there, he had prevailed.

Wearing disapproval like a shield, two of them had stood by while he'd struggled out of the leathers with the help of his buddies. The ordeal had left him slightly cranky. And in significant discomfort.

He was, however, considerably cheered by the presence of his two friends.

The pair, John-Parker in his cowboy boots and hat, and Brandt looking as cool as J Crew in a plaid button-down and red-laced hiking boots, stood next to the emergency room exam table.

Rio lay on said exam table wearing a faded hospital gown and waiting for a doc to read his X-rays while the trio caught up a bit. Not that they could cover fifteen years in a few minutes, but he let them do the talking while he listened. It wasn't that he didn't trust his "brothers." He did. But with his top-secret clearances, he was duty-bound never to say too much.

He was impressed to learn that John-Parker and Brandt co-owned and operated a successful personal security business, and he already knew JP, as he called the multi-named buddy, was getting married.

"JP found a woman to put up with him for the long term. What about you, Brandt? Didn't you vow never to enter this town again? Only a woman could be the cause."

The quieter foster brother grinned. "Can't argue. I found a good reason to move back home."

JP elbowed him. "Yeah. Her name is Berkley Metcalfe."

Rio smirked. "Why am I not surprised? Daddy's little rich girl took you back, huh?"

"She did. And she's going to marry me next summer."

A surprising pinch of envy hit Rio. "All my rowdy friends are settling down."

"You're next."

He shook his head. "My life is not the lifestyle for a family."

"Which brings us to the question. Where have you been since we last saw you—what?—ten, eleven years ago. And what have you been up to?"

Before he formulated a vague reply to questions he didn't want to answer, especially in a public place, the door swooshed open and a scrubs-clad doctor sailed in, white coat flapping. He carried a pair of X-rays that he shoved into clips above a lighted screen.

"Your diagnosis was correct," Doc said without preliminary. "Both fibula and tibia sustained simple fractures." He poked a finger at the spot. "Right here. See that white line. Shouldn't be there." He poked a finger at another bone. "That one either, although it's not weight-bearing."

Wasn't as bad as he'd thought. No weight-bearing bones. He could walk right out of there.

"So I'm good to go then." Rio started to sit up.

"Not quite. A simple fracture means the bones remained in place. However, the tibia *is* weight-bearing and requires treatment. Four to six weeks normally. We'll fit you with a removable boot cast for showering but absolutely no weight bearing for at least the first four weeks. Let's recheck in a couple of weeks to see how you're healing."

Rio frowned. This was not in the plans.

"I'll be gone in four weeks." He hoped. Surely, the op investigation wouldn't take more than a month. Would it?

The doctor gave him a long look. "See me before you leave, and we'll get you transferred to your preferred doctor."

"Right. Sure." A simple fracture. He'd be fine in a couple of weeks max.

The doctor clicked off the x-ray light. "Remind me again how this happened."

"Lay my Harley on its side. Slammed into a curb."

"Why?"

"I was attacked by a pack of dogs pulling an elf in a Santa hat."

As Rio had intended, the doc laughed. "That's one I've never heard before."

"Dogs and Christmas. That's Eden in a nutshell," JP said.

Eden. Pretty name. As in "The Garden of," Rio supposed.

"What my smart-mouthed friend is attempting to say, Doc," JP added, "is that Eden is a dog groomer. She was walking a bunch of dogs that decided to have a runaway."

"In the middle of the street. Right in front of my new Harley."

"Eden Carnegie?" The doctor glanced at Rio for confirmation.

Rio shrugged.

"One and the same," Brandt said. "You know her?"

"Everyone knows Eden, don't they? The spirit of Christmas in the flesh. She's already hit me up for a donation to this year's veterans' party."

His two buddies nodded. "Got us, too. She's small but mighty, and when it comes to her veterans, she's a force of nature."

A party for veterans? What was that about?

"The dimples get me every time. And she's always smiling, no matter what." Doc shook his head. "My wife says I'm a pushover for any good cause."

Dimples. Yeah, Rio'd noticed. The smile, not

so much. Even with her eyes filled with concern, the deep cheek indentions flashed anytime Eden's mouth moved. In his line of work, he was trained and paid to noticed the most insignificant details. And there was nothing insignificant about the dimpled elf in the Santa hat.

His thoughts surprised him. Here he was with a broken leg due to Eden and her dogs, and he was having a semi-mushy thought about her. Maybe he'd hit his head as well as his leg.

"Give us a few minutes and we'll fit you with the boot and a pair of crutches." Before Rio had time to argue, the doc swept out of the room.

Before the door sucked shut, the elf in the Santa hat swirled through it. The energy in the room rose several notches. Hadn't it? Or was he suffering hallucinations brought on by an undiagnosed head injury?

Eden, the dimpled elf, rushed toward him. "What did the doctor say? Are you okay? What can I do to help? I am so sorry. Lucky has never done that before."

He held up his hand to stop the barrage of words and the concern in her lash-rimmed eyes. "I'll heal. Who's Lucky?"

"The handsome boxer who caused all the commotion. He's really a big baby, the sweetest boy. I'm obedience training for a client, so I can't believe he misbehaved like that. He's been doing so well."

"Don't worry about it."

"Oh, I don't worry. I pray." She flashed those

entertaining dimples. And, as Doc said, the smile lit up the room. "What does the doctor say about your leg?"

He flicked a hand. "Tiny little crack. Nothing serious. I'll be up and running in a few days."

JP snickered. Brandt looked at the ceiling and shook his head.

Eden caught their drift. "It's worse than you're saying, isn't it? Will you have a cast?" Her big eyes widened. "Surgery?"

"No surgery." Although surgery might be preferable. They'd knock him out for a day or two and he'd stop noticing this woman's dimples and giant brown eyes that looked as soft and warm as chocolate pudding. Shiny, too, from the inside out, as if she'd swallowed a hundred-watt light bulb.

"A cast then. How long do you have to wear it?"

He shrugged. The injury was nothing except irritating. "Boot cast. Four to six, Doc says. I'm shooting for two."

"Long time to sit around playing video games," JP said. "You should volunteer with Eden's veterans' group."

He didn't *play* video games. He lived them.

"That's a grand idea." Eden lit up brighter than the lights on Main Street. "Would you?"

"Doubtful. Won't be here that long." He hoped.

Brandt's cell phone buzzed. He glanced at the screen and excused himself.

"Me, too," JP said, holding up his phone. "I'd better call Zoey and give her an update." To Rio, he said, "I'll be in the lobby when they finish with you."

"Check on my Harley."

"Will do."

Rio nodded his thanks.

As soon as they left, Eden launched into a description of a huge celebration she and a band of like-minded souls organized for the nearby veterans' home. A *Christmas* celebration. Veterans, he could do. Christmas, not interested.

They probably stuck Santa hats on the poor old guys and sang "Jingle Bells" ad nauseam, too.

Face bright and dimples dancing as she flashed the occasional excited smile, Eden finished on a high note with the promise of presents for everyone, the reading of the real Christmas story—whatever that was—and maybe even a visit from Santa!

Rio had the powerful urge to say, "Bah humbug."

Instead, he said, "Nice of you, but I don't think so."

He was saved from continuing the conversation when a nurse came in carrying the tools of his forthcoming misery.

"Let's get you fixed up and out of here," she said to Rio. "Doctor left orders that I'll go over with you, and physical therapy is headed over with your crutches."

"Great." Not.

Eden, whose Santa hat wiggled when she moved her head, said, "I should go." She dug in her jacket pocket and offered him a business card. "Call me if you need help with anything. I'm serious. I feel bad about what happened, and I'm good at running errands or cheering people up."

He could see that.

"Or—" she flashed those dimples "—if you change your mind about volunteering."

Neither of those things was likely to happen.

Rio took the card and nodded anyway.

When she left the room, the energy seemed to leave with her.

Intriguing woman. Who loved Christmas.

No thanks.

Eden's afternoon was filled with appointments. After fixing a quick lunch for Grandpa, she headed to the shop next to the house where she conducted her dog grooming business.

In one corner of the salon, Brinkley kept an eye on the proceedings from his red, sleigh-shaped bed. With K-love Christmas playing over the computer, Eden bathed and trimmed nails for a Rottweiler, trimmed nails for a couple of walk-ins, fully groomed a pair of poodle sisters and performed a between-groomings brush and condition on an Aussie mix. All clients except the Rott received stretchy red bow ties and a doggie treat. Rosco the Rottie preferred a red-and-green-plaid bandana. As he proudly trotted out the door with his owner, he looked handsome and ready for the holidays.

After the day's last client departed, Eden began the usual routine to clean and disinfect the salon.

Her thoughts returned to the eventful morning that had thrown her behind schedule. She glanced at the clock. Past seven and she still needed to prepare dinner for herself and Grandpa before visiting Mom at Golden Leaves, the memory care facility.

But she wasn't complaining about her busy schedule. She was thankful. Even though Mom's memory faded more all the time, Eden was grateful to still have her in her life. And Grandpa was her rock and best buddy.

"Ready for dinner, Brink?" The funny little mixed-breed dog hopped up, tags jingling as he shook himself. *Dinner* was his favorite word. Two years ago, he'd come to her from the animal shelter, ragged fur matted, loaded with fleas, shy and depressed. She'd seen the sweetness in his worried eyes and had fallen in love.

She flipped the sign on the door to Closed, clicked on the outside multicolored lights she'd had up since the beginning of November, adjusted the "Merry Christmas" wreath, then locked up and went inside the home where she'd grown up.

The warm scent of cooking greeted her.

Tossing her money bag on an end table, she moved through the living room into the kitchen. "Grandpa?"

The old man stood at the stove, stirring a skillet. "How about my special goulash with a salad for dinner?"

"Sounds wonderful." She crossed the room and kissed his cheek. "You're energetic today."

"Feeling good. Only had two coughing spells all day."

She frowned. "Did you use your breathing machine?"

He waved her away. "As the doctor ordered. Now, set the table like a good girl and let's chow while you tell me about this morning's adventure."

The long sentence was too much for his severely damaged lungs. He had another of his "coughing spells."

Eden guided a chair beneath him and hurried to his bedroom for an inhaler. While he used it and caught his breath, she set the table, poured two glasses of tea and dished up the goulash.

"I'm okay now. Let's eat."

Holding to his arm, Eden helped him out of the chair and supported him to the table. He was overweight, which exacerbated his breathing problems, but the same lung condition made exercise nearly impossible. A no-win situation.

He sat down with a tired exhale. "Aggravates me to be a worn-out old burden."

"Grandpa, you could never be a burden any more than Mom and I were burdens to you after Daddy died."

"Different deal. I was lonely and grieving, too. He was my only child. You and your mother were all I had left of him. I needed you." He paused for a few breaths. "Having the two of you to look after kept this house from feeling empty. Though these days, you're the one doing the looking after."

"I can't get along without you, Grandpa. Don't ever think you're a burden. You're my rock."

After Dad was killed in the Middle East, she and Mom had moved in with Grandpa. Only in the past year had her mother's Alzheimer's forced the decision to a residential care facility. Eden had fought the move, wanting to care for her at home, but early in the diagnosis, Mom had made her own arrangements.

After they said grace and filled their plates, Eden said, "If Mom's having a good day, I'll bring her for a visit on Sunday."

"You still going over to see her tonight? It's getting late."

"I won't stay long. She asked for a new puzzle and I found a good one at the dollar store that she doesn't have."

Nodding, he took a giant scoop of goulash onto his fork. "Now, what's this about some maniac motorcycle rider trying to run down my granddaughter?"

He sounded like the gruff police officer he'd been for many years.

Eden forked a bite of tomatoey meat and macaroni, chewed and swallowed before responding.

"My fault entirely. The man was coming down the main road on the edge of town, minding his own business, when the noise must have upset Lucky and he jerked me and the other dogs into the street. I got tangled in the leashes, fell and couldn't get up fast enough. If the rider, who you might remember, by the way, hadn't thought fast, we'd all be hurt. Instead, he hurt himself to avoid hitting us."

Grandpa's forehead furrowed. "Who is he?"

"Rio Hendrix. He was one of Mamie Bezek's foster sons."

Frown disappearing, Grandpa chuckled. "Oh, yes, I remember Rio. Ticketed him a few times for speeding. I often wondered if the boy had a death wish."

After serving as an MP in Vietnam, Grandpa had hired on with the local police department. Her friends had both feared and respected him. He'd been firm but fair.

"His leg is broken, Grandpa, because of me and my dogs. I want to do something nice for him. He needs cheering."

The old man patted the back of her hand. "Sis, you could make a statue smile. I'm sure you'll think of something. 'Tis the season to be merry and no one is merrier than you."

Eden sat up straighter. "Grandpa, you're a genius."

A plethora of holiday-themed ideas flooded into her mind. If nothing else, she could take him a gift of Christmas!

Eden pushed the chair away from the table and stood, suddenly in a rush. "Thank you for dinner. I'll do the dishes when I get back from Mom's. Love you."

She kissed the top of his still-thick graying hair. He smelled like shampoo and aftershave, an indication that he'd had a good day indeed.

Thank you, Lord!

In the morning before her clients arrived and after working with Star and Lucky, she'd go shopping. Afterward, she'd find out where Rio Hendrix was staying and pay him a visit.

Christmas presents made everyone feel better.

Chapter Three

The hotel room proved adequate for a man on one leg and a crutch. Everything was close together, although this proved to be a different kind of problem since Rio didn't like to be confined. However, this would have to work until he could ride again.

Rio hobbled to the window and pushed back the curtains, letting in the day, an overcast one. Down below, beyond the sparsely populated parking lot, some joker had lined the front of his business with inflatable snowmen and other holiday characters. Was that a penguin? A big green Grinch?

"I feel ya, buddy," he muttered. He and the Grinch had the same attitude about the Christmas sham.

The whole display was ridiculous. Overkill. A meaningless effort and expense. Half of the inflatables had deflated or fallen over in Oklahoma's incessant wind.

Across the way, strings of flashing multicolored lights were visible along the various businesses. Like most of the small towns he'd ridden through in the past few days, Rosemary Ridge couldn't wait to profit off people's Christmas fantasies. He knew from long experience that wishing for something didn't make it happen.

Rio hopped to the easy chair and resumed reading the book JP and Zoey had brought over last night from Miss Mamie's collection. If he stuck around town, he'd need more books, preferably thrillers or nonfiction, but Orwell's novels were worth a second and third read. They gave him food for thought. Orwell had been closer to correct than most Americans knew.

His old friends had urged him to stay at the foster home with Brandt and the boys or with JP in the rental he was about to move out of, but Rio had declined, needing his privacy to think and, if he were honest, to brood about what was happening with the investigation.

If he was to be stuck doing nothing for days on end, unable to ride his Harley, he didn't want to wear out his welcome. The three street rats had been apart a long time. They didn't know each other that well anymore.

But, man, it had been good to see them. Those two had their lives in order, thriving in business and personal relationships. Brandt was even adopting a kid, his baby brother. Rio could hardly wrap his head around that one, but he was happy for his foster brothers even as he envied them.

Not that he was the settling kind. And he sure wasn't anybody's daddy. Kids deserved a dad who knew how to love. His only example had been an intellectual control freak who'd ruined every special occasion, especially Christmas, which he'd declared was for those lacking enough mental acuity to recognize that they'd been manipulated and brainwashed into believing a farce. A Hendrix was too intelligent for that; a hypocritical statement on his father's part given the stupid things he'd ultimately done.

Rio drew in a long, frustrated sniff.

Life was tough, ugly, dark. If his childhood hadn't proved it, his years as an intelligence operative had.

Must be the painkillers making him maudlin. Although ibuprofen—the only drug he ever took—wasn't known to be mood-altering.

Picking up the novel, he refocused on the intense, cautionary plot of *1984* and wondered how a man in the 1940s could so accurately envision today's troubled world. Interesting stuff. Orwell, an intellectual to admire.

When a knock came at the door, Rio figured the visitor was Brandt or JP. Who else except housekeeping?

Grabbing the crutches he'd leaned against the chair arm, he hoisted up and made the short journey.

Juggling crutches while unhooking the chain took a second, but he managed to unlock the door.

Outside stood the elf, the effervescent one—Eden-something—wearing the same Santa hat and a bright red sweater embossed with a fuzzy brown reindeer.

He almost closed the door in her cheerful face, but her beaming smile was so sincere and eager, he hobbled backward, opened the door wider, and let her in.

A shopping bag and dog leash dangled from one arm. In the left hand, she carried an enclosed food container, one of those foam carryout boxes. In the other was a disposable cup of what smelled like fresh coffee. Trotting beside her, the small, homely dog from yesterday bore the same happy attitude as Eden. The woman was contagious, even to a dog.

"Zoey told me you were here. I hope you don't mind." She flashed those dimples again. "I brought muffins and coffee."

"Thanks."

"Do you like banana nut? They're homemade, fresh this morning. But extra special because I decorated them."

He hadn't eaten a homemade muffin in years.

"Decorated? With what? Sprinkles?" She was definitely the kind of woman who'd want sprinkles. Glitter, too.

"And a few other things."

Rio hitched his chin toward the small table next to the window. "Mind putting them on the table? I'm still learning to use these crutches and carry stuff at the same time."

She did as he asked, unloading the shopping bag, too. "How's your leg? Does it hurt much?"

"No." Not if you didn't count the ache that had kept him awake most of the night. "Just annoying."

Rio remained standing, expecting her to leave right away, but she lingered, lighting up his room in a way that opening the curtains hadn't.

With an inward shrug, he figured a distraction was not a bad thing. He was bored anyway. And Eden was kind. Pleasant to look at, too.

Wobbling to the table, Rio eased himself down on one of the two chairs, careful not to put weight on the bad leg. One of the crutches tumbled to the floor. Eden snatched it up.

"I came to apologize again." She stood over him with the crutch.

Feeling ornery, he eyed the crutch and teased, "Are you planning to whack me with that unless I forgive you?"

"What? Oh." She laughed and stepped back to place the crutch beside the other. "No. But I *would* like your forgiveness. Lucky is sorry, too."

"The dog? He told you this?"

"He did. He moped all the way home. His owner said he cried in his sleep last night. Poor baby. I think he had a nightmare."

Rio's mouth twitched. She had a sense of humor. He found humor appealing in people, especially women. Not that he was there to get involved with a woman. Especially a Christmas junkie who smiled all the time and had probably never had a care in the world.

"No apology needed," he said. "You can tell that

to Lucky." He eyed the small terrier-looking mutt at her side. "Toto, too. No hard feelings, pal."

Eden beamed. "Rio, meet Brinkley. Brink, this is Rio, the man you licked yesterday."

Plopped on his tiny bottom, Brinkley lifted a paw.

Rio leaned forward to shake the dog's hand.

"Charmed, I'm sure," he said, amused by both woman and dog.

"Brinkley's a therapy dog. I take him to the veterans' home. Some of the guys call him Toto, too." She shrugged. "Dr. Colter says he has cairn terrier in his lineage. Along with some other breeds."

Rio had never owned a dog even though he liked them. His lifestyle wasn't exactly conducive to pet ownership.

Eden pushed the coffee toward him. "This is black, but I have creamer and sugar in the bag."

"Black's good." He took a sip. Pretty decent coffee.

Eden flipped open the muffin box and used finger and thumb to place one on a napkin in front of him.

Rio stared at the decorated muffin. "Are those Christmas lights?"

"Not real ones, of course. Just M&M's perched on their edges and joined together with a strip of green icing. I didn't have time to get too fancy."

Looked pretty fancy to him.

"Cheerful, aren't they?" she asked. "Cream cheese icing goes great with banana muffins. I hope you like them."

He took a bite. His tongue thanked him. And her. "Nice."

He sipped his coffee and took another bite. The woman knew her way around a muffin. He wondered if she cooked other things.

Scratch that thought. He cooked. He was a good cook. Mostly he ate out.

"In that case—" She opened the shopping bag and began pulling out items. "I brought you a Santa hat. Everyone needs one."

He hiked a doubting eyebrow.

She smiled as if his reaction tickled her.

"Or would you rather have this?" With a flourish, she extracted a headband complete with sparkly wobbling snowmen atop a pair of antennae. They made him think of the silly inflatable display.

"Or this? Ta-da." Like a magician with a rabbit in a hat, she produced another headband, this one topped with padded brown reindeer.

They were both so ridiculous, he nearly choked on his muffin. "Please, you're torturing me. Stop." And he meant it.

"One more thing."

Groaning, he held up a hand. "No."

She flashed that smile. Her eyes sparkled. "Maybe two."

"Stop." But he laughed when he said it. She really was entertaining.

"The pièce de résistance." Hers was the worst French accent he'd ever heard. And being a fluent speaker of the language, he'd heard plenty.

Rattling the shopping bag for effect, eyes dancing, she whipped out a miniature Christmas tree crammed with too many fake bells, candy canes and baubles.

"Gaudy."

"I know," she gushed. "Isn't it wonderful? It even lights up!"

"Wonderful." Just what he didn't need. Reminders of the worst times of his life and the man who'd caused them.

If his inside showed on the outside, he'd hurt her feelings. No matter how misguided, she was trying to be kind. Rio attempted to keep his face clear of expression, but must have failed.

Eden's chipper countenance crumbled. "What's wrong? You hate it?"

He actually felt bad about telling her. "I don't really do Christmas."

"Why not?" Her puppy-dog eyes widened. "Oh." She pressed a hand to her lips. "Did I offend you? Is it a religious thing?"

Him religious? "No."

She blew out a breath. "That's a relief. I never want to offend, but Christmas is so wonderful and joyous and beautiful, sometimes I go overboard."

He snickered, eyeing the paraphernalia she'd scattered on the hotel's table. "You? Overboard?"

The smile returned. Her eyes sparkled. "You laughed, didn't you?"

He had. For a few minutes, her ridiculous display

of unmitigated Christmas cheer had made him forget the worries eating a hole in his guts.

She tilted her head. "Is there a reason you don't like Christmas?"

He hadn't said that exactly, but it was true. Christmas brought back too many bad memories. "Bogus holiday."

"Well, that's sad."

Sad? It was common sense. Why get all bent out of shape for a few weeks out of the year over a commercialized holiday with no meaning other than to increase crime and domestic violence?

"Didn't you have Christmas when you were a boy?"

Inwardly, Rio flinched. "Something like that."

"Maybe you'd like Christmas if you experienced a really good one." She sounded so hopeful, he sort of hated to disappoint her. "Helping others celebrate always lifts my spirits."

If her spirits got any brighter, she'd disappear in a burst of light. He'd never seen anyone smile so much.

"I wouldn't mind having another muffin," he said, more to change the subject than because of hunger.

She gave him a long look as if she knew what he was doing and then pushed the box toward him and pulled out a chair to sit. The little dog raised both paws on her knee but she told him to sit. He did.

Arms folded on the tabletop, Eden said, "I remember you from high school."

"Yeah?" He also remembered her, now that he wasn't in the throes of wrecking his Harley and breaking his leg.

Mary Poppins. Pollyanna. Goody Two-shoes. He'd heard her called all those names. Eden had been the perpetual cheerleader type although she'd never actually *been* a cheerleader that he'd known of. She'd have been a good one. "You were a couple of years behind me, weren't you?"

She nodded. "My grandpa remembers you, too."

"Who's your grandpa?"

"Steven Carnegie."

He stopped with a muffin midway to his mouth. "The cop?"

"One and the same."

He put the muffin down and chuckled. "Tell him I'm innocent. I wasn't speeding this time."

"I did." She waved a hand. "He's retired now anyway. He hasn't handed out a ticket in a long time."

"He was a good cop."

"Nice of you to say that considering the tickets he gave you."

"I earned them." He picked a red candy off the muffin and popped it in his mouth. "You were in my Spanish class one year, weren't you?"

"Mrs. Framer's class, yes. *¿Habla Español, Señor Rio?*"

He rattled off a short paragraph in Spanish and was surprised when she interpreted it correctly.

"Good memory. Impressive."

"I have a Spanish-speaking friend," she said. "Sometimes we speak in Spanish, so I don't forget for those times we go on mission trips with the church. But if memory serves, you learned so fast, Mrs. Framer let you read Spanish novels while the rest of us were still learning basics."

Rio shrugged. "Languages aren't hard once you figure out the patterns. They're like math."

She made a gagging sound. They grinned at each other.

Eden Carnegie was cute, entertaining, and even with the ugly reminder of a Christmas tree staring at him, had proved to be a pleasant distraction.

They continued talking about high school, segueing to the small town and the changes he'd not yet seen.

He didn't know how much time had passed but suddenly her cell phone chirped. After a quick glance, she made a face and stood. "I have to go. I have an appointment in ten minutes."

"Doggy bath?"

"Marquita, the Chihuahua with stinky breath but really kind brown eyes, is coming in for her regular appointment. Teeth brushed, toenails painted, the works."

"Fun times."

"Oh, it is. I love my job." She gathered up her dog and went to the door.

"Thanks for the muffins, et cetera." Rio cast an uncertain look at the fake tree perched in the center of the table. It was doomed for the trash can.

"Oh, almost forgot." She rushed back to the table, dug in the sack and extracted what appeared to be a shopping list.

The paper was folded in two. She plunked it in front of him then went to the door and opened it.

He didn't want her to leave. A shock, but there it was.

"What is this?" he asked, mostly to delay her.

"You'll see." She flashed a final grin and shut the door behind her.

Rio opened the notepaper, scanned the list and couldn't decide if he should laugh or get mad. The woman was relentless. Cute but relentless.

At the top, she'd written, "Must watch. Guaranteed to lift your spirits."

At the bottom was a list of Christmas movies.

Sure. Right. As if a movie could erase a lifetime of bad experiences.

Eden applied perfumed conditioner to the shivering Chihuahua at the doggy mom's request and began the quick process of gently blow-drying Marquita's clean fur. A regular client, Taffy Robbins was a photographer and good friend who volunteered on the Celebrate Veterans committee.

Taffy documented every detail of Marquita's spa treatment with her ever-present camera.

"I'll email these to you," she offered. "You can use them on your website and social media if you like them."

"I'd love that." Eden handed Taffy a candy cane

from the clear apothecary jar. "Do you remember Rio Hendrix from high school?"

Taffy's eyes widened. "The gorgeous blue-eyed bad boy? Yes. Like half the girls in school, I had a killer crush on him at one time."

"He's back in Rosemary Ridge for Zoey and John-Parker's wedding."

"Is he still as handsome as he was in school?" Taffy unwrapped the candy cane and took a bite from the tip. The crunch caused Brinkley to sit up.

"Maybe more so. Maturity looks great on him."

"Oooh, I'm glad I'm photographing the wedding reception. He'll never know how many shots I take of his pretty face." Taffy patted a hand above her heart. "Eye candy. Better than this kind of candy. But don't tell Chad."

Chad was Taffy's latest boyfriend, who'd lasted longer than most of them.

"Chad's a nice-looking guy." But Eden couldn't argue about Rio's looks. The man *was* very handsome in a dark, dangerous, Heathcliff kind of way. But she'd made him laugh. After she'd injured him. "I broke his leg."

"What? Eden!" Taffy's raised voice caused Marquita to cower. She quickly changed her tone to baby talk. "Not you, Precious. Mummy loves her baby girl."

Eden stretched a small red ribbon and bow around Marquita's neck while she shared the accident with Taffy. "This morning I baked him some muffins and gave him a tiny tree to spruce up his hotel room, but I still feel terrible. He'll be on crutches at the wedding."

"You say he intentionally wrecked his bike to avoid hitting you?"

"He did."

Taffy pretended to swoon. "What a hero."

"A hero who doesn't particularly like Christmas. He said he doesn't *do* Christmas. He was less than excited about the decorations I gave him. He called them torture." But he'd laughed.

"If he's a grinch, he's certainly come to the wrong town."

"I know, right? He said his objection wasn't due to religion, so I think he must have had a bad experience."

"Or two. Remember, he was one of Miss Mamie's foster boys. We don't know what his life was like before he showed up in town, too cool for words and smarter than the teachers."

"That's true. I hadn't thought of that. Miss Mamie was the kindest soul and she celebrated, so whatever turned him off must have happened before he came to live with her." Eden picked up the dog and nuzzled her. Marquita smelled great now, even her breath. "I asked him if he'd help with the veterans' Christmas party."

"I'm taking pictures for that, too! What did he say?"

"I think the word he used was *doubtful*, but I talked to John-Parker this morning. He promised to bring the topic up to Rio again when he wasn't in pain from me breaking his leg."

Taffy squinched her eyes together. "Ouch."

"Yes. Exactly. If not for his quick thinking, the dogs and I would have been badly injured, maybe killed. Instead, he hurt himself."

"Gotta love a man like that." Taffy handed over her credit card and shrugged into a fringed jacket.

Eden ran the card and returned it, along with the tiny dog.

After Taffy left, Eden checked her schedule. She smiled when she saw that one of her favorite clients was due any minute. Moose, the beautiful Irish setter with the endearing personality, and his people, the Colters. Jake Colter was one of the town's two veterinarians who sent her lots of clients. He and his wife, Rachel, had had a baby boy earlier in the year, so Eden wasn't surprised when Dr. Colter and his young daughter, Daley, were the ones who dropped off Moose.

While they discussed today's grooming needs, Eden's cell phone buzzed inside her pocket. She'd made a policy never to interrupt a client to answer the phone, so she ignored the call for the time being.

After Dr. Colter and Daley departed, she extracted the cell phone to take a look. The number wasn't familiar but they'd left a voice mail.

She dialed her mailbox and listened. A deep male voice hummed pleasantly in her ear. She recognized the appealing baritone. Rio Hendrix.

"I have a question. Call me." The line went dead.

Eden looked at Moose. The setter, perched on his bottom, cocked his head to one side and whacked his long tail against the concrete floor.

"I wonder what that's about?" She didn't wonder long before the phone rang again and she was busy juggling clients, appointments and a call from the memory care center concerning her mom that drove every other thought right out of her mind.

Chapter Four

The fifteen-minute drive to Golden Leaves Memory Care was long enough to allow Eden's panic to begin to subside. Pulling into the parking lot, she bolted from her compact SUV and made a dash through a cold drizzle to the entrance.

Adrenaline still pumped through every blood vessel. Her fingers shook as she tapped the security code into the door panel, listened for the snick and yanked the door open.

She couldn't believe this had happened. In the two years Mother had been at Golden Leaves, she had never wandered away.

Sally, a familiar nurse met her in the foyer.

"Have you found her? How did she get out without being noticed? What happened?"

Sally placed a calming hand on her shoulder. "The director just called. He found your mother walking about a block from here. They're stopping for ice cream before heading back."

Eden tipped her head toward the ceiling, eyes closed, and let out the breath she hadn't known she was holding. "Thank you, Jesus."

"Apparently, Helen thought she was on her way to Friendly's Custard Shop."

"But that's in Rosemary Ridge, fifteen miles away." Oh, how she hated this awful disease.

"Yes. Thankfully, we noticed Helen's absence very quickly and she didn't get far."

"How did this happen? It cannot happen again."

"At this point, we aren't sure, but we are doing a very thorough investigation that has already begun. One of the aides saw her going toward the kitchen and assumed she was getting a snack."

Freedom for Mom to move around the facility and choose her own food and snacks was one of the reasons Eden had agreed to Golden Leaves. But safety had been the main draw. Golden Leaves had a top-notch reputation as one of the best memory care facilities in southern Oklahoma. The full staff, various in-house therapies, regular physician visits, art, music, recreational activities and events, and even their own hair and nail salon, made the enormous price tag worth the extra hours Eden worked to make the monthly payment.

"Has this ever happened before with any other resident?"

"I've been here as charge nurse for twelve years and this is only the second time. But, in our estimation, two times is too many. We are better than this."

Twice in twelve years. A good track record. But still, with an Alzheimer's patient, the danger was ever-present.

Sally motioned toward a hallway. "Come into my office to wait. We'll chat with the other staff to see what we can learn. Georgina, Melinda, come with us, please."

With the staff members following, Eden accompanied the nurse into the tidy office near the main entrance reception desk.

They'd barely taken their seats and begun to discuss the situation when the door opened and Eden's mother entered. The director was right behind her.

"Mama!" Eden sprang from the chair and rushed to envelop in her mother in an embrace. When she pulled away, Mom stared at her with a blank expression.

Eden's chest constricted. "It's me, Mom. Eden."

A painful heartbeat ticked before the fog cleared and her mother's eyes refocused. "Well, of course it is. You've changed your hair again."

Not in a long time. "You never liked the highlights."

"I didn't, did I? I still prefer your natural brunette, but you're pretty no matter what you do to your hair." Mom turned toward the gathered listeners. "Isn't she the prettiest little girl?"

Tenderness softened Eden's voice. "Mom."

The others smiled and nodded.

"Your daughter is lovely, Helen," Sally said, "like her mother. Did you enjoy your ice cream?"

Mom blinked a few times and Eden could see she was fighting to remember.

"Mom, listen to me." Eden took both of her

mother's hands in hers. "You aren't supposed to leave the facility by yourself. Please don't do that again. Someone would have given you a ride."

A tiny frown appeared between Mom's eyes. "Mr. Richardson drove me to the ice cream shop. I had strawberry cheesecake."

"Is that why you left the building? To get ice cream?"

Asking all these questions was probably too much, but sometimes they enjoyed a perfectly rational, grounded conversation.

Mom tugged her hands away and twisted them together. Agitation elevated her voice. "I was supposed to meet Jeremy at Friendly's, like we always do on Friday. They said he wasn't coming, but he never misses."

The sadness dug deeper. Today was Tuesday. And Daddy had been killed when Eden was twelve. "Your date night."

Her mother's face took on a glow. "He'd rush to meet me and hurry into the shop, smile wide, carrying flowers. Sometimes he'd leave work early and buy me Gerbera daisies. I love daisies."

"I know. Daddy loved us, Mom."

"We never missed our night out together until… until—" Her expression crumbled. Tears started to flow. "I miss him so much, Eden."

Eden, heart heavier than a school bus, opened her arms and let her mom decide if she wanted a hug. Helen walked into her embrace and sobbed against her shoulder.

As she held the woman who'd once held her, Eden whispered a prayer for her mom and strength for herself.

This was life with an Alzheimer's victim.

The House of Hope foster home for teenage boys brought memories rushing through Rio's brain, although the old house with the cracked, faded linoleum was now an updated, modern home. JP and fiancée Zoey had improved and expanded every inch of the place.

The only truly recognizable piece of furniture was the kitchen table; a rectangular wooden structure still bearing the scars of boys wielding forks and knives. Somewhere underneath the table, his initials were probably still visible.

Around the table and to the left at a big island, he counted ten people besides himself. JP and Zoey. Brandt and his lady love, Berkley. Zoey's two small children and four teenage boys. Brandt's baby brother, Nicholas, slept fitfully in a baby seat on the floor next to Berkley. That Brandt was now the guardian of an infant from his troubled past was still a shocker Rio couldn't yet wrap his head around.

He remembered Berkley Metcalfe, an upper-crust blond beauty who appeared high-maintenance. From the looks of her hair, clothes and nails, she still was, but, she'd always been a nice person, even to the dregs of the earth like him, a street rat. He was impressed to learn that she'd eschewed a lucrative business partnership with her wealthy father in favor of working in the foster-adoption arena for the state. That she loved his old pal Brandt and the baby she couldn't keep her hands and eyes off, was obvious.

Zoey was new to him, but from first impressions, she seemed all right. A good match for JP and a strong housemother for the teens and her two littles. Even though she was much younger, her personality reminded him of Miss Mamie. Velvet steel.

Conversation bounced from one person to the next as they ate dinner. Rio quietly observed; a skill he'd acquired in his operative work. *Look and listen, and carry a backup plan if something goes south.* Not that he worried about that here. Force of habit.

"Rio, what are your plans while you're recovering?" Berkley dabbed at her gorgeous face with a paper napkin. "Besides the big wedding, of course."

JP answered for him. "We're trying to get him involved with Eden and her veterans."

Berkley brightened. "The Christmas party is a wonderful event, and she can always use more help."

Not from him.

Besides, Eden had never returned his phone call. For the best, perhaps. Her glow-in-the-dark smile and positive personality made him itchy. They had to be fake. Like Christmas.

Ignoring an inner vision of deep dimples, Rio swallowed a bite of the tastiest enchilada casserole in remembrance and tried to focus on that. "Can't. Broken leg. No transportation."

Brandt snorted. "Excuses. I never expected to see the day when a tiny thing like a broken leg would slow down Rio Hendrix."

Rio managed a smirk. "I'm getting old."

Fact of the matter, he felt older than everyone at the table, even though the adults were in the same age bracket. A man who'd seen and done too much got old in a hurry.

Nothing to do with healing his bones though.

"One of us can drive you into Centerville." Brandt went on. "They've got a car rental place. Much as I liked my rental, I turned it in there when I decided to stay in Rosemary Ridge."

The teasing look of love Berkley centered on Brandt was radiant. "And bought a brand-new Corvette at the Chevy agency down the road. Poor baby had to settle for a different color blue."

"I wouldn't mind driving one of those myself," Rio said.

One of the teenagers slung a wad of long dark hair back from his face and mumbled, "Me neither."

"Your day will come, River," Zoey said. "Once you and the guys get that old Ford fixed up, John-Parker's promised to teach you to drive."

"Yeah, yeah, promises." The boy, whose cynical attitude reminded Rio a little of himself, shoveled a fork of Spanish rice into his mouth and stared down at his plate.

The adults exchanged glances before Brandt continued the conversation. "I can squeeze out the time to drive you to the rental place."

"Can you drive with that boot on?" Zoey asked Rio.

"His left leg is broken, Zoey, not his right," JP said. "He can drive anything except his Harley and a stick shift."

Rio was tempted to growl. Or howl. He wanted back on that Harley so bad, he'd risk reinjury if he wasn't concerned a bum leg would affect his job. The one he could lose at any moment.

"Sounds good. Are they open late?" He did not like depending on anyone, not even his buddies, for transport. A rental would suffice for now.

Brandt shook his head. "Don't think so. Let's shoot for first thing in the morning."

"We taking your Vette?"

A grin lit Brandt's face. "Absolutely."

"Great," Rio said with a matching grin. "I'll drive."

Eden blew a lock of hair out of her eyes and put Lucky through his paces again, walking the Boxer sans leash, at heel around the fenced-in backyard. Rock music blasted from an old boom box she'd owned since her teenage days, the noise intended to inoculate the dog so that he'd never again have a run-away. Earlier she'd played traffic noises, including motorcycles and sirens. Lucky hadn't flinched.

The training days since the incident appeared to be successful.

She checked her phone for the time. A few minutes until nine when her first grooming client was scheduled.

Since long before sunup, she'd been at work on one endeavor or the other. The to-do list for the Christmas party was complete, as was the budget. The two did not match up. Yet.

Eden prayed that would change soon. *Very* soon. Although she couldn't think of a solution.

Before coming out to work with the dogs, she'd also created a list of phone calls she needed to make and shot off several emails to ask, once again, that the veteran services she'd invited to the event would RSVP. Some had, some hadn't, and she wanted them all there. The next volunteer meeting was on Saturday and she hoped to give them an update. She'd sent her small team of volunteers an email of the lists, asking for help to complete the tasks.

Busy morning, and it wasn't even nine yet. Since she was almost finished with Lucky for the day, she'd have a minute to check on her grandfather and make sure he was set up for the morning.

To Lucky, she commanded, "Sit." Lucky plopped down, ears erect, golden eyes hopeful.

She patted his brawny head and offered a treat. "Good boy. Good Lucky. Now, stay."

She held out a hand in a stop-sign gesture and backed away. When she reached the chain-link fence, she dropped her hand. "Release."

The big animal charged toward her—thrilled with himself—and would have jumped had she not held out her hand again. "Down."

To her delight, Lucky obeyed. Another day or two and he'd graduate. And she'd get paid. More funds for the party.

"Is this the beast who broke my leg?"

At the unexpected male voice in her backyard, Eden squeaked and spun around, hand to her suddenly pounding heart.

Rio Hendrix stood just inside the gate leading to the outside and her front yard.

"You startled me. I didn't hear you drive up." She blinked a couple of times. "Wait?" She shot out a hand. "Did you drive? Not your Harley."

Beneath the dark beard, Rio's lips curved. Slightly. Leaning on his crutches, left foot off the ground, the noticeably handsome man hitched his head toward the unseen driveway. "Rented a car."

She hurried to turn off the boom box. Sweet peace and quiet settled over the yard. She almost sighed in relief.

"You can drive?"

"Apparently." He held his hands out to each side but kept the crutches under his arms for balance. "I'm here."

Yes, he was.

All six-feet-whatever of tall, dark and movie-star handsome, the black-lashed swimming-pool eyes drew her attention like magnets. He'd trimmed his dark beard to a close crop. Very appealing. As was seeing him standing upright.

Eden's smile appeared. She couldn't help it. "I'm so happy to see you up and about on your own. This is awesome!"

"Feeling pretty good about it myself." Crutches swinging in easy rhythm, he came closer.

"The hotel room closing in on you?" Eden bent to reconnect Lucky's leash. The boxer inched closer to Rio, probably in apology.

She gave him credit for trying and brownie points to Rio when he dropped his hand, palm open, toward the dog.

Lucky inched forward and nuzzled the offered hand.

"Something like that." He absently massaged the side of Lucky's face. "I've hung out with JP and Brandt the last couple of days but don't want to overstay my welcome. You know what Ben Franklin said about company."

She didn't have a clue. "Uh, no. He was a philosopher. I recall that."

She also recalled that Rio Hendrix had a brain big enough to hold an encyclopedia. Or in today's world, Wikipedia. Maybe the entire internet. He could probably personally program Alexa.

"*Poor Richard's Almanack*. Paraphrased, but Franklin said that after three days, company, like fish, begins to stink. And I've had my three days."

Eden laughed. "Whatever happened to old-fashioned hospitality? I really don't think John-Parker or Brandt would consider your visit stinky. Zoey told me they are delighted to see you and catch up after all this time."

"Can't argue. It's great to be with them again." A smirk of humor appeared. "But I don't want to stink either."

A car door slammed. Eden glanced at her phone. "Awk, that may be my next client, early." She led Lucky to an outdoor kennel to await pickup from his owner. Rubbing his ears, she said, "See you tomorrow, boy."

The dog looked toward Rio and whined.

Eden turned to see the man next to the outside gate as if about to leave. Had he wanted something in particular? Or just to assure her that he was all right?

The latter thought warmed her. She smiled at him. "Would you like to come inside and see my shop?" Maybe give her an opportunity to recruit him for the party?

He shook his head, eyes hooded as if he had a secret—which he probably did. Lots of them. "You didn't return my call."

Eden clapped a hand to her mouth. "I had an emergency and completely forgot. I'm sorry."

He shifted his stance, adjusting the crutches as if he was about to step toward her again. "Emergency? Everything okay?"

"Yes. Thanks." No point in going into the episode with a virtual stranger. Mom was safe. All was well.

"Eden?" a voice called from her left. "You have a customer."

Pivoting, she spotted Grandpa at the back door, holding the storm door wide.

With a wave, she said, "Thanks, Grandpa. I'll be there in a minute."

Grandpa exited the house, taking the two steps slowly. She needed to install a handrail. "Who's your friend?"

Ah. So that was the real reason he'd opened the door. He didn't recognize Rio and, ever protective, was keeping an eye on her. The peace officer in him hadn't quite retired for good. Not when it came to looking after his granddaughter, regardless of her age. And Eden loved him for it.

Before she could formulate a reply, Rio set his crutches into long, quick strides and crossed the yard toward her grandfather.

Upon reaching the older man, he extended his hand, again balancing on the crutches. "Rio Hendrix, sir. Good to see you again."

"Rio. Oh, yes, my granddaughter told me about the accident." Grandpa's gaze scraped over the crutches and boot cast. "Thank you for what you did. Putting yourself in harm's way to protect her and the animals. That's a real man in my estimation."

"Instinct, sir."

"Good ones, I'd say." Grandpa squinted. "Military?"

"Of sorts."

"I see." Grandpa nodded sagely as if he knew exactly what Rio meant. Eden certainly didn't.

"Grandpa, Rio," she said, "I'm sorry to interrupt but I have to get to work."

"Go on, sis. We're big boys." Grandpa waved her off. To Rio, he said, "Coffee's on. Want to join me?"

He pushed the door open wider.

To Eden's amazement, Rio followed her grandfather inside the house.

Chapter Five

Rio stood at the hotel window staring out at the afternoon. This morning had taken an interesting turn. He hadn't had the chance to talk to Eden the way he'd planned, but he'd enjoyed the two hours over coffee and pancakes with Eden's grandfather.

The former law dog was still mentally sharp, but his physical condition made Rio acutely aware of his own vigorous health. Broken leg excepted. His injury would heal. The old man's would only worsen until the oxygen he'd worn during their conversation would no longer be enough to keep him alive.

Life was cruel.

Hopping back to the chair, Rio looked at his cell phone and pondered the call he needed to make but dreaded. This would be the third time he'd tried since returning to the States.

He found the number in his contacts. His finger hovered above the green phone icon.

A man who'd fearlessly lived with and sabotaged some of the most dangerous men on earth right under their noses shouldn't be nervous.

"Don't be a coward," he muttered darkly. Rejection doesn't kill the body, only the soul.

He jammed his finger against the icon.

A very short four minutes later, he pushed End.

Anger mixed with disappointment pulsed through him as he mulled the conversation with the prison. Yes, they'd received the funds he'd sent to his dad's phone account as well as Rio's visitation request form. For the fourth time this year. Yes, they'd received his background check and security clearances. Unfortunately, inmate Hendrix had refused his request for both phone calls and visitations.

Again. And again. And again.

But what had he expected? Carlton Hendrix wanted to punish him, and every time he returned a letter or denied a visitation request, he did exactly that. The old jerk must be gloating. Pleased that he'd hurt the boy who'd betrayed him.

Rio tossed the phone onto the table and scrubbed both hands down his face. He wanted to kick something.

The idea brought a grim chuckle.

"Go ahead, break another bone, idiot," he muttered.

He'd developed a strong aptitude for remaining calm under pressure, unfazed by the madness swirling around him. Nothing shook him. Not even a bomb going off in the next building, something that had happened to him twice.

His dad was the only human being with the

power to unsettle his cool demeanor and cause him to question himself, his intellect, his abilities, his memory.

Even now, all these years later, the questions ate at him. Who was the guilty party? His dad? Or him?

Most of the time he kept the questions at bay. When on assignment, he was too busy plotting, thinking, managing volatile and possibly lethal situations. Coming home to the States brought back the things he'd left the country to avoid. Coming to Oklahoma exponentially multiplied the overthinking.

A major problem of having a high IQ—the brain never rested, not even in sleep.

Mood darkening by the moment, he shoved up from the chair, grappled with the crutches to hobble back to the window. Eden was right. This place was closing in on him.

Eden. The effervescent one.

This morning he'd driven to the address on the business card she'd given him. By following the raucous blast of music he hadn't recognized, Rio had discovered Eden and the big boxer in an enclosed area between her dog grooming shop and the back of her home—an older ranch-style he remembered as belonging to her grandfather, a local cop. The shop was new, at least to him.

He'd observed her for a couple of minutes, impressed by her work with the dog but also appreciating the sight of her. The December morning had been cool, but she'd worn only a white, puffy vest over a long-sleeved pink shirt and denim jeans. Dark hair slicked back in a ponytail, she'd looked like a teenager. A petite teenager.

After the accident, he'd thought her too small to lift his Harley. She'd fooled him. Lots of strength in that petite package.

When she'd noticed him, the smile and dimples had appeared. Were they the reason he'd driven over there? To see someone who didn't appear to have a care in the world, a woman who exuded joy in contrast to his dark moods?

He swiveled on his one good foot toward the small table and the ugly Christmas tree she'd given him. The Santa hat and headbands still lay where she'd placed them, next to the wadded list of Christmas movies she'd suggested would cheer him.

He huffed, wished he had a dog to talk to, picked up the silly snowman headband, imagining Eden wearing it. She probably would just to make someone smile.

Had he ever been that carefree and childlike?

Someone that happy couldn't have a care in the world. Was her life all sunshine and puppy dogs?

"Must be nice." He hoped nothing ever came along to steal her rose-colored glasses.

With a pinch of envy, Rio wished he could erase half his memory.

But he was who he was. He'd made his choices, and once a person succumbed to the dark, he could never find the light again. A hard lesson for a twelve-year-old, but innocence lost could not be regained.

He tossed the headband toward the small, hotel trash can, then gathered the other items into one hand and dumped them, too.

Leaving the reminders of the bogus holiday for housekeeping, he hobbled out of the hotel to his rented car. Not a Vette like Brandt's as he'd considered. A man in danger of losing his livelihood couldn't overspend, although his savings and investments from hazardous pay were a nice cushion if the axe were to fall. Instead, he'd chosen a slightly more reasonable Mustang in his preferred sleek black. A convertible, of course, with all the trimmings.

Oddly, he'd wanted Eden to see the car this morning, wanted to take her for a ride and watch her reaction. He'd been slightly disappointed that she'd been too busy. Only slightly. A woman like Eden was not his type. *At all.*

Regardless, he'd let the top down and thought of her riding in the passenger's seat, ponytail blowing, laughter ringing out.

Would she ride with him? Or call him a maniac for driving an opened convertible in winter? Would she realize a convertible was significantly warmer than a Harley and he'd ridden the bike across the country?

Rio huffed a short self-deprecating laugh. She'd probably call him a maniac for the Harley, too, if she had the chance, and ask if he had a death wish.

Her grandfather had mentioned the same this morning, although he'd joked when he'd said it, as they'd reminisced his multiple fines for speeding.

It wasn't the first time someone had used the term in reference to him.

Rio wondered if they were right. He wasn't chasing death, but he *did* enjoy the satisfaction of outsmarting the bad actors of the world even when doing so put him in significant danger.

Interesting that he'd never suffered a broken bone or a serious injury until he'd encountered a certain little elf and her pack of cheek-licking dogs.

Amused by the thought, Rio tossed the crutches into the passenger side of the car and slid onto the smooth black leather to start the engine. The temperature gauge lit up. Fifty-three degrees. No wind. Even with the overcast sky, the weather was not bad.

Giving a quick tug to the overhead lever, he tapped the button to electronically lower the top, buckled his seat belt, and enjoyed the sweet engine as he rumbled out of the parking lot.

Wind in his face. The open road. Forget his problems for a while. Real freedom.

Main Street in a small town was hard to avoid and this one was a wall-to-wall explosion of Christmas. The side streets, he soon discovered, were just as bad. As if in competition to see who could produce the gaudiest display, every home sported some nod to the holidays. Even Mamie's house. With help from JP, the now-domesticated rabble-rouser Zoey and the teenage boys had strung lights on every eave, window and bush. A giant uniformed nutcracker stood sentry next to the blue front door.

The trouble was, all of the Christmas hoopla put Rio in mind of Eden Carnegie. Again. Miss Congeniality. Not that he minded thinking about her. She was by far the best option in his mental repertoire.

He considered another trip to her shop and wished he had a dog that needed grooming. He always went into an op with a cover story and more than one backup plan. A dog would be perfect this time.

The thought made him chuckle.

Eden wasn't an op. She was a pleasant woman who, he was slightly bothered to admit, attracted him.

But not bothered enough to avoid her.

In his business, he never knew what lurked around the corner or which day would be his last. *Carpe diem.* Seize the day. Grab the moment.

Eden interested him and that was excuse enough to see her. Their shared interest in veterans was an added bonus.

He'd given considerable thought to her work with older veterans and wanted to know more, thanks to some state-of-the art nudging from JP and Brandt. What exactly did she do for the old vets besides the Christmas gig? Listen to war stories? Bake them cookies?

He chuckled. "Yeah, or muffins with M&M's for lights."

She never had returned his call.

However, she *had* invited him inside to see her doggy salon. Yet another excuse to drop in on her.

Making the turn on Hampstead Street, Rio followed the line of bedazzled, twinkly houses to the section of older modest homes and Eden's Dog Grooming Salon.

The sign on the door, right below the Christmas wreath, said, "Come In. We're Open," so he twisted the knob and hobbled inside.

The smell of strawberries hit him in the nose. The sight of Christmas overload punched him in the gut. That and the image of Eden in a Christmas-red smock massaging liquid into the coat of a white poodle.

She glanced up, blew a lock of hair from her forehead and showed him her dimples. "Hi."

"Hi." Now what?

Oh, right. Right. Veterans. Had he addled his brain so badly in the bike wreck that one minute in her company stole his thoughts? "You're busy."

"Always, but I like company while I work." The dimples flashed at him again. Was she always happy? "This girl is Ingrid. She's a standard poodle who comes in every four to six weeks for me to keep beautiful." Eden leaned close to the dog's face and, in baby talk, said, "You are a pretty girl. Yes, you are."

Rio sniffed the air. "Strawberry shampoo?"

"Conditioner. Ingrid has dry skin, especially this time of year, and she likes to smell and look pretty."

"Very French of her," he said.

Eden completed the massage and reached for a towel hanging to the side of the large industrial sink. "To what do I owe the pleasure of seeing you twice in one day?"

He arched his eyebrows. "I'm a glutton for punishment?"

The statement had the effect he wanted. She laughed. "You *are* in dangerous territory, mister. Me, dogs, leashes." She nudged her chin toward one wall and a selection of dog supplies—leashes, collars, toys, treats and more. Even doggy Christmas sweaters. "All we need is a motorcycle."

She flashed him that smile again and if Rio hadn't spent years learning to control his reactions in dangerous situations, he would have lost focus.

Not that she was dangerous. Not his usual type of danger anyway.

Something about her, however, energized him.

The gloom of his father's latest rejection began to ease.

The dog salon reminded him of its owner. Cheerful. Cute. Friendly.

Dog posters lined empty spaces. One showed a Jack Russell Terrier in a joyous running leap with the caption, "Live like somebody left the gate open."

Good advice. For a woman like Eden.

His gate had to remain closed at all times.

Crutches under his arms, Rio moved around the salon, taking in the other details. The building was packed but well organized and housed an extra room he couldn't see into.

A shepherd woofed at him from one of three crates adjacent to the front door.

"Hush, Axel. He's a friend."

Was he? Maybe. For certain, Eden was easy to be around, comfortable in who she was. A friend he wouldn't mind having.

"Customers in waiting?" he asked of the two crated dogs.

With practiced motions, she gently patted Ingrid's curly locks and stood her on a floor mat to shake. The dog was good-sized, maybe fifty pounds, but Eden lifted her with minimal effort.

Admirable.

"Yes," she said, "the Yorkie's next and then Axel. His heavy coat requires extra time, and he hasn't been here in a while. Misty, that's the Yorkie, is easy peasy."

Easy peasy. She was the kind of American woman who would use the term. Everything in her life seemed to be easy peasy.

Except, he thought with humor, crossing the street with a handful of dogs.

"Talked to JP..." he started.

She tilted her head in a quizzical expression. "JP? Oh, you mean John-Parker? I've never heard anyone call him JP before."

As noted, the poodle wasn't small, but Eden lifted her onto a towel-covered table. Every male muscle in his body wanted to help, but he'd probably lose his balance and fall on his face. A pretty thought.

"She's a big dog. Sorry I can't help. At the moment."

"Not your job, Rio, but thank you for the

thought." She settled the compliant poodle in a simple restraint and began to brush out the face and ears. "You were about to say something about John-Parker."

"Right. He told me about this veterans' thing you do. Thought you could use my help."

"You're a veteran, right?"

"Yes." No point going into his complicated military and government background.

Her gaze dropped from the poodle she was now blow-drying to his booted foot. "The big Christmas party is my area of greatest need, and you don't *do* Christmas. Wasn't that what you said?"

Yeah. He'd said that, and he'd meant it. But today he was bored out of his skull.

"I like veterans." *And you.* "Can we start there? What do you do exactly?"

She turned off the hair dryer and faced him. "Tell you what. Meet me at the veterans' home in Centerville tomorrow afternoon at one thirty and I'll show you."

He was hoping for something sooner. Like a ride in his Mustang after she closed up shop.

"Tomorrow at one thirty?" He narrowed his eyes as if thinking through a busy schedule, knowing full well he had nothing to do. Nothing. And he, a man of action, was climbing the walls—metaphorically speaking, of course, given the condition of his leg. "Let me check my calendar."

As if reading his mind, Eden laughed. "I'll text you the address."

* * *

Every Wednesday afternoon, Eden cleared her appointment schedule and closed the grooming salon at noon. After lunch with Grandpa, she and Brinkley headed to the Centerville Veterans Living Center, fifteen miles from Rosemary Ridge.

Some days, a friend or two accompanied her, but today, others had begged off. The holidays kept everyone overly busy.

Except Rio Hendrix. She'd texted him the address. He hadn't responded. Would he show up?

She had to admit she'd enjoyed both of his visits to her home, however brief. Something about him drew her. Maybe the secrets in his eyes or perhaps his solemn intensity. She knew him to be brilliant, knew he had a sense of humor, had seen his protective side. But sadness hung over him like a dark cloud. She'd noticed it every time they'd met, but especially when he'd come to the shop. As if he carried a heavy load he couldn't let go of.

Eden wanted the world to be happy, especially at Christmas. And if Rio wasn't, were she and the dogs responsible because of the accident? Was he simply eager to get well and move on? Or was there underlying darkness inside the man?

Snapping Brinkley's leash into his cheerful red-and-green harness, she settled a tiny Santa hat onto his fuzzy head and looped the soft elastic under his chin. "There. All ready to spread some Christmas cheer, aren't you, Brink?"

As if he knew exactly what she meant, Brinkley

answered with a short yip and turned his black button eyes toward the veterans' home. He loved coming to the facility, especially to soak up all the extra attention the residents gave him.

Adjusting her own Santa hat, Eden set out across the parking lot to the long, brick building and waited to be buzzed inside.

The scent of today's lunch hung in the air, though she couldn't recognize the specific source.

A handful of residents in the mostly male center gathered in a large open living room furnished with comfortable chairs, recliners, two round game tables and the odd wheelchair. Some looked up when she entered and waved in greeting. She knew them all by name and greeted them as she moved into the space with Brinkley.

From his wheelchair, Clyde, a grizzled Vietnam vet like her grandpa, patted his remaining leg. "Let me see that good boy."

"He's eager to see you, too, Clyde." She bent to unleash Brinkley, whose entire body wiggled faster than a washing machine on spin dry. "No treats today, please."

Clyde grinned. "Aw, spoilsport." He patted his shirt pocket. "I saved him a bite of chicken from lunch. Baked. No grease. It's good for him."

So, chicken was the lunch smell. "Okay. One little bite, if he's a good boy."

"He's always good, aren't you, Brinkley?"

At Eden's hand signal, the dog leaped lightly onto Clyde's lap. The man received his share of cheek kisses before Brinkley settled quietly against him. Clyde stroked the freshly washed fur over and over.

Instinctively knowing what each human needed, Brinkley had passed his therapy training with ease. The veterans loved him and she was confident they enjoyed the dog's visits as much or more than hers.

"That new feller says he's with you. He your man?" Clyde's free hand motioned toward the corner table where four men were deep into a game of dominoes.

Eden's heart leaped. Silly thing. Rio sat at the table, studying a row of game pieces in front of him with an intense stare.

"I didn't know he'd already arrived."

"Been here all morning. Says he was an army ranger. Wes Verona in Room 7 was, too. You might tell your fella that. Seems like a good man. He better treat you and this pup right or he'll answer to us."

"Oh, he and I aren't—we're just—" What were they? Friends? Acquaintances? Attacker and attackee? "Did you say he was an army ranger?"

"Didn't you know that?"

Eden stared at the domino table and the dark head bending over a cross pattern of dominoes. A ranger. No wonder he appeared intense. "As I said, we're just acquaintances."

"Ah, well, that's too bad. I like him. Keep him anyway. See where it leads."

With an amused shake of her head, Eden moved on to visit with others. After a few minutes, Brinkley joined her to work the room like the professional people-lover he was.

Eden's glance kept returning to Rio. Finally, as if he felt her gaze, he looked up, caught her eye and held on.

Warmth surged through Eden, though the feeling was nonsense brought on by Clyde's assumption.

Rio tipped his chin upward and then turned to speak to the other domino players. To a man, the three faces looked at her and grinned.

With lithe ease, Rio rose from the table, reclaimed his crutches and came to the couch where she sat watching one of the residents play with Brinkley.

"I got your texts." Rio leaned the crutches against the couch arm and settled next to her. The couch gave toward the center and their shoulders touched before he readjusted his position.

At his nearness, Eden's cheeks warmed, a silly, annoying, schoolgirl reaction. "You didn't reply."

And, she realized, she'd wanted him to. Just as she'd wanted him to hang around the salon the other day. Was it because he was undeniably good-looking? Or because she had the powerful urge to fix him, to lighten him up? Perhaps even convince him that Christmas and faith in God were good things.

Maybe all of the above. And she was okay with that.

"What exactly," Rio said, "does a man say to a GIF of dancing candy canes dressed like reindeer? Complete with googly eyes."

So he *had* read her texts. And he'd seen the funny Christmas GIFs she'd sent to make him smile.

"Weren't they cute? I thought they'd get your attention."

He snorted. "Mission accomplished."

Eden shifted her position, turning slightly to meet his laser-intense gaze. "Thank you for coming today. Clyde said you'd been here awhile."

He lifted one shoulder in a lazy shrug. "These are my people."

"Clyde said you're an army ranger."

"Was. Who's Clyde?"

She pointed out the man now kicked back in a recliner and reading a newspaper.

"What do you do now? If you're no longer a ranger."

"I'm on a leave of absence." He drew her attention to his boot cast. "In case you didn't notice, Santa broke my leg."

That told her nothing. Was he avoiding her question? Or was she invading his privacy?

"So," Rio said, "what else do you do here with the vets?"

"This is it. We talk, and I listen, or if one of the guys needs a ride somewhere, one of the other volunteers or I take them. Most of the men have regular doctor's visits and prefer to go with a family member or one of us. Mostly with us."

"Why's that?"

"Why do you think?" She gave his shoulder a bump with hers. "We're more fun!"

He smirked. "Muffins? Santa hats? Dancing reindeer?"

Seeing the humor in his eyes, she batted her lashes at him. "When the occasion warrants."

"What do you do for an encore when it's no longer the holidays?"

"There is always something to celebrate."

"Yeah?"

Eden widened her eyes at him. "Yeah."

Was she flirting with the guy? Was he flirting with her? Did she want him to?

To cover her consternation, Eden stood and handed Rio his crutches.

"Come on, oh ye of little faith. Wes, in Room 7, was a ranger, too. He'll want to meet you."

Something flickered in Rio's expression. Only a small flicker but enough to make her wonder once again about the secrets hidden behind the cool facade.

Chapter Six

It was after six, darkness closing in, when Rio walked Eden and her little dog out of the veterans' home. Charming streetlamps illuminated the center's circle drive and the big red bows tied around each post. Red Christmas lights alternated with white on rounded evergreens that lined the sides of the building.

The holiday season in small-town America. He couldn't escape it. The room of every veteran Eden had taken him to displayed a tiny fake Christmas tree, complete with garish decorations. Compliments, he surmised, of Mary Sunshine herself, who must begin her cheerful campaign long before Thanksgiving.

Rio had to admit some of the more sterile, barren-looking rooms had needed *something*. Men, like him, with no family. No loved ones. Only a kind heart like Eden to acknowledge they were human and still alive.

Spending time with them got a man to thinking about his own future. Would he end up in a place like that someday?

From foster home to veterans' home. Alone.

If he lost his job, what would he do in the interim?

Rio swung the crutches from the sidewalk to the step-down driveway. Eden was next to him. He liked having her there. Wanted to prolong their evening.

Yeah, he told himself. *He needed the distraction.* And Eden's positive energy.

Even if he wasn't suffering from a troubled mind and a restless soul, Eden interested him.

They'd had little time today to share conversation with each other. He had, however, observed the way she interacted with the men and admired the genuine friendship she gave each one. She never pandered or condescended, and he appreciated that. The guys, too, recognized her genuine interest. Almost as if they were her granddad, too.

Nice woman. She had no business with him. If she knew who he was, the things he'd done, the secrets he held inside and the ones he'd take to his grave, she wouldn't want him there. Would she?

Rio slanted a look toward her. In the dusky twilight, a lapel pin on her sweater caught the light from an overhead lamp they passed. A small, colorful cameo of the nativity scene.

"Nice pin," he said.

Eden dipped her chin toward her shoulder. "Thank you. It's very special to me. My dad gave this brooch as a gift to my mother years ago, and she recently passed it to me."

"An heirloom then." Something he would never own.

"Oh. Well, yes." She stroked two fingers over

the pin. "I guess you could say that. If I ever have a child, it will be theirs someday."

Car lights swung onto the circle drive. Though impeded by the crutches, Rio shifted positions so that his body blocked Eden's from the oncoming traffic. Instinct, from years of service. He'd already scanned the area for threats, another long-engrained habit.

"Why isn't a nice person like you already married?" he asked.

She turned to the right, where he supposed her car was parked. He didn't know what she drove, other than a pack of dogs on leashes, he thought with humor.

"I could ask the same of you."

"I asked first."

Eden showed him her dimples. Even in lamplight, he had trouble taking his eyes off them. Off her. If he didn't want to stumble and fall flat on his nose, he'd better get control of his rambling eyeballs.

"All the usual excuses." Eden ticked them off like a list she'd memorized. "I haven't met the right guy. Not many single men patronize my business. No one's asked."

He snorted. "I don't believe the last one."

She stopped in midstride to face him, head tilted in a charming pose. There went his eyeballs again. He narrowed them in self-defense.

"Why, Mr. Hendrix, was that a compliment?"

"Yes, and an indictment against the single males

in this state. You can't tell me you don't have a boyfriend."

"Forty-seven at last count." She aimed an index finger and a grin toward the building behind them.

He enjoyed her humor. A lot. "Which one do you think will propose first?"

Eden's eyes sparkled up at him. "I'll let Brinkley choose."

As if he followed the conversation, the dog's fuzzy head swiveled back and forth between the humans.

The little creature had brought comfort and cheer to a lot of people today, and he seemed to know it.

Rio felt pretty good about the afternoon himself. At the same time, he was painfully aware that this was the kind of place he'd someday live out his life. Alone. Frail. Delighted to have someone, anyone, to talk to.

A few of the residents lived in the facility with a spouse, and some had mentioned families who visited on occasion, but most, having outlived their relatives, were alone. Like him.

He had no relatives—one of the reasons the government had recruited him for secret intelligence operations. His mother had been an only child and his father—well, that side of the family had washed their hands of him when he'd sent his father to prison. The Hendrix clan had left him to rot in the social services system.

Eden touched his arm. "Why the scowl? Did I say something I shouldn't have? Are you sorry you came?"

"Not at all. It's not them." And she sure wasn't the problem. "The men are great. Today was an eye-opener, a reminder."

"Is that a good thing or a bad thing?"

"Jury's still out." He managed a half smile.

"I was hopeful you'd want to come back again."

"I do." He and the veterans had plenty in common and the men loved to talk. All he had to do was listen. Anyone could do that. And should. Visiting the old guys was something to do while he awaited a decision from headquarters. "I will."

Eden emitted a tiny squeal of joy and squeezed his upper arm.

You'd have thought he'd handed her the keys to a brand-new car.

Which put him in mind of the Mustang.

"Are you hungry?" he asked. "We could grab a bite."

Uncertainty darkened Eden's brown eyes. She pressed her fingertips to her lips.

She didn't want to go. At least not with him.

He thought they'd established a friendly give-and-take during their time together, but maybe not. Maybe he was losing his ability to read people, a skill that had saved his life and his covert ops more than once.

Not that an invitation to dinner was life and death, but he liked Eden Carnegie. She brightened the world around her, around him.

He started to retract the invitation when she

spoke. "I'd love to, Rio, but let me call Grandpa first. Okay?"

He'd forgotten about her grandfather.

"Sure."

The call was brief but when the conversation ended, she held up an index finger. "One more call. Sorry."

"No hurry." He had nowhere else to be. JP and Brandt, his only pals, weren't even around. They were both out of town on security assignments, jobs he envied at the moment.

He'd heard nothing at all from his bosses.

While Eden spoke to someone named Sally, Rio bent to rub Brinkley's kinky fur, at the same time cataloging every word of the conversation even as he appeared not to be. Force of habit.

"All set," she said as they continued through the parking lot. "I'll meet you there. Wherever we're going."

"Ride with me." He jerked his head in the direction of his parking spot. "Mustang convertible, top down."

She stopped in mid-step. "Seriously? In December?"

Rather disappointed in her reaction, Rio shrugged. "We can leave the top up, if you'd rather."

"Are you kidding me? No way! Let me grab our jackets from the car. Brinkley and I love convertible rides!"

"Even in December?" he asked to be sure.

"That's the best time of all!"

Rio's disappointment flew right out into the shadows. The effervescent one was on the job, ever ready to give the world—and him—a reason to smile.

As night closed in, the temperature dropped, but Eden didn't mind. Apparently, neither did Rio as he drove the sports car smoothly through the streets.

"Where to?" One hand slung casually over the steering wheel, he flicked his gaze toward her. "Are you starving? Or up for a longer ride?"

"Food can wait." She clapped her hands in a rapid staccato and gave a silent squeal of excitement.

"I was hoping you'd say that." Humor danced in Rio's blue eyes. "Old highway?"

The old highway that once connected Rosemary Ridge with Centerville and other towns was rarely busy anymore. As teenagers, the old highway had been a favorite hangout and drive spot. Lovers lane, too, for some.

"Perfect. Turn the music up and fly." She poked a finger at him. "Within reason. No speeding tickets."

"Spoilsport." White teeth flashed and she had the distinct feeling that he'd drive exactly as he wanted to, regardless of the danger of a ticket. Was he a daredevil or, as Grandpa said, a man with a death wish?

Maybe both since he'd been an army ranger.

"Don't worry. You're safe with me. Promise."

She was about to find out if that was true or not.

The man certainly carried an air of danger. Oddly, she had no fear. At all. Not after observing his interactions today with the veterans. Respectful, kind and genuinely interested, he'd drawn out each one until they talked to him in a way they'd never talked to her. Man to man. Vet to vet.

The connections made sense. Although the veterans liked her, she'd never been in the military. She couldn't fully understand what they'd experienced. Rio did.

After a bit, she had slipped out of each room and left them alone, aware of how meaningful their conversations were.

Beneath Rio's air of danger and secrets lived a good heart. At least when it came to veterans.

Aware of Rio in a fresh way, and unusually happy to spend this time with him, Eden zipped her jacket to her chin and settled against the plush leather to enjoy the ride. Brinkley, in his hooded sweater, perched in her lap, mouth open, tongue flapping, ears erect after she'd connected his harness through her seat belt.

The wind in her face and hair was cold, and she loved it. Rio seemed impervious, his shaggy black hair as wild as hers. Brinkley was in his element.

When they reached the old highway, Rio nodded to the radio. "Find your favorite station and crank it."

She did, and when Rio heard her choice, he groaned. "I should have guessed."

In spite of his grumbles or maybe because of them, Eden burst out in a hearty duo with "Deck the Halls," giving special emphasis to the "fa-la-la-la-las."

Rio kept looking at her as if she'd gone off the deep end, but she saw the sparkle in that look and transitioned smoothly to "Rudolph the Red-Nosed Reindeer" and then to "Jingle Bells."

Believing he'd had a bad experience somewhere along the line, Eden was determined to show him how wonderful and fun Christmas could be under the right circumstances. Jesus's birth was worth the effort.

When Brinkley decided to join in the singing with a howl worthy of his distant wolf ancestry, she burst out laughing.

Mouth curved, shaking his head, Rio turned down the volume. "Do you know every Christmas song on the planet?"

"Yes!" Then she laughed again. "Most of them, anyway. Mom loves Christmas, too, so, when I was a child, we always had carols playing from Thanksgiving onward."

He hiked a doubting eyebrow. "You wait until Thanksgiving?"

"No, no. *Mom* waited. *I* don't."

Rio snorted. "Figures."

"Surely, you know this one. You speak Spanish!" Eden turned up the radio. "Come on, sing. No one but Brinkley and me will hear your awful voice."

He shot her a quick glance. "Who said my voice was awful?"

"It must be," she teased, "or you wouldn't be afraid to use it."

"I see what you're doing there. Goading me into participating in your Christmas nonsense."

She pressed a palm to her chest. "I am, indeed, an expert goader. Come on, sing with me. I promise not to tell anyone that you succumbed to my goading."

His nostrils flared. "You sing. I'll listen."

"Coward."

Eyes going dark and hooded, Rio turned his full focus to staring down the dark highway, silent.

Had she offended him?

She lowered the radio's volume. "Rio, I was joking."

"Feliz Navidad" suddenly didn't seem so merry.

"I know." He flashed her a glance. "Hasn't all your...exuberance worked up an appetite yet? Where should we eat?"

His mood shift put a damper on her singing, but by the time they reached the burger joint, the topic had turned to favorite foods. She'd been fascinated to learn he'd spent most of his adult life overseas and had eaten a wide variety of cuisines she'd never heard of, including several foods that made her grimace.

Over made-to-order burgers and fries, she teased him about eating raw octopus and he retorted with, "Better than stink bug nuggets."

"Oh, stop! You're ruining my burger. No one eats that." She grabbed for her glass of water.

He chuckled, apparently delighted at grossing her out. "You've never been to Africa, have you?"

She shook her head. "Have you?"

"Worked there half of my career."

"Doing what? Are you still in the military?"

"Five years as an army ranger."

A hedge if she'd ever heard one. "But you're not anymore?"

Elbows on the table, he spread his hands in question. "What is this? Twenty Questions?"

"Sorry." She waggled a French fry in apology. "Just making conversation."

"Fair enough." He regained his burger. "I guess you could say I'm a government contractor."

That still didn't tell her anything. "Doing what?"

Rio tilted his head back and chuckled. Eden, like most people, was, as she'd said, only making conversation. These past few days he'd had to remind himself more than once that no one in Rosemary Ridge was a terrorist, a spy, or an intelligence contact. They were friendlies.

Although he was adept at lying—a necessity in the spy business—Rio didn't want to lie to a woman who interested him as much as Eden did. He could concoct a cover story and she'd believe him. But he didn't want to. Not that he felt the least guilty for lying under certain circumstances, but truth, even a hint of truth, was always preferable. Poorly chosen lies could come back to bite him.

So, accustomed to sliding around sticky conversations with enough truth to be believable, he pumped his eyebrows and jokingly repeated the popular spy-movie line. "If I tell you, I'll have to kill you."

As he'd hoped, Eden, as innocent as a newborn lamb, took the bait. "Okay, I get the message. Whatever you do is private and personal and you don't want to talk about it."

Actually, he did want to talk. A real dilemma. He simply couldn't. "I've had some issues with my bosses lately. Talking won't fix the problems."

Eden sat straighter, a picture of earnest concern. "Are you in danger of losing your job?"

"A possibility." He kept his tone calm and nonchalant, as if he didn't really care one way or the other. Another carefully honed cover. "Isn't that the nature of any well-paid job? We never know when the company will downsize or go another direction."

Neither of which applied in his case, but the false impression proved effective.

"That's awful. I'm sorry."

He lifted one shoulder in a carefree shrug. "It is what it is."

"One of the great things about being self-employed," Eden said, "is that I am not likely to fire myself." She widened those sparkling brown eyes. "And my boss, the skinflint, refuses to give me a raise. No danger of being too well paid. Or of losing my job!"

He allowed an easy smile, wishing he could say the same. Not about the pay. The pay was fine if putting his life on the line every day had an equitable price tag. But the danger of losing the only world he fully understood and fit into stuck like a chicken bone in his throat.

Eden's small hand snaked across the tabletop and touched the tips of his fingers. "Don't worry, Rio. Everything will work out for the best."

Her touch sent an interesting charge along his skin. "Hope you're right."

"Romans 8:28. I believe that verse with all my heart."

She'd lost him there. "I don't know much about the Bible."

"'And we know,'" she quoted with a happy twinkle, "'that all things work together for good to them that love God, to them who are the called according to His purpose.' Whenever I hit a roadblock, I quote that promise to myself and trust that God will work out even the stickiest situations for my ultimate good. It's my life verse."

A life verse? Interesting term. He supposed his "life verse," if he could call it that, was from military intelligence. "In God we trust. All others, we monitor."

Although he didn't actually trust in God that much. Fact was, his trust meter ran on danger alert at all times.

As he pondered her easy reference to her Christian beliefs, Rio took another bite of his fast-disappearing burger, chewed and swallowed.

"That could be a problem," he said.

"What could be?" With dainty care, she dabbed

a napkin at the mustard in the corner of her ever-tilted lips.

A fascinating mouth, if he'd ever seen one. He had to drag his traitorous eyes away. Was her faith in God the reason for her unrelenting optimism?

A faith he did not share.

From his viewpoint, things only worked out well if he made them. Sometimes even his efforts proved fruitless. "I'm not sure I believe in God. At least, not a useful one."

If he'd slapped her, Eden wouldn't have looked more stunned. Her eyebrows pinched together, eyes concerned. Either for God or for him.

If a man could snatch words out of the air, Rio would have.

"Why not?" she asked, her voice soft and troubled, as if she cared about his soul.

Did he even have one anymore? If he did, it was black as onyx.

"Long story. Mostly, I wasn't raised in any kind of faith. Parents weren't believers." And eleven years in very bad places made him question if any god existed for the good of humankind.

"But you lived with Miss Mamie, and she was a believer."

"Science always made more sense."

Eden leaned her elbows on the table, steepled index fingers bouncing against her chin as she held his gaze with her earnest one. "Did you ever stop to think that the two go hand in hand? Science *is* God."

Her tone was sincere, based on faith, not logic, so that Rio regretted the conversation even more. He didn't want to shoot down her logic with a debate he could win, so he hedged. "I don't think I ever heard it put that way."

"Then give it some thought in that smart brain of yours. Be open-minded. You'll see."

He doubted he'd see anything but a fairy tale. But he took another bite of burger rather than argue. He appreciated the joy that clung to her like perfume. No use dimming her light.

"Tell you what," she said, smile reappearing as she leaned back against the booth. "I'll pray that everything works out for you on the job. When it does, will you believe that God exists and that He cares about you?"

Rio narrowed his eyes, teasing, determined to push the conversation back onto more comfortable ground. Religion made him think of too many unpleasant memories, of his dad, his mom, of the dangers to anyone espousing Christ in foreign lands where he'd lived most of his adult life. "Are all Christians this sneaky?"

With a twinkle in her eyes, she waggled a ketchup-tipped French fry. "Hang around and find out, my friend."

He could do that. Not that he had a lot of choice. Nor a lot of hope.

A thousand prayers to her God wouldn't stop the decisions of the United States government.

Chapter Seven

The following Friday evening, six volunteers, plus Eden and Brinkley, gathered in the meeting room of the Rosemary Ridge Library to finalize plans for the Celebrate Veterans Christmas Party. The group included librarian Ramona Estes, Taffy Robbins, Rachel Colter, Rachel's mother, Sue, who volunteered for everything in town, and Wink and Frank Myrick, who never missed an opportunity to know what was going on.

Brinkley had made the rounds to receive a head rub from each member before taking his place on the floor next to Eden's chair.

"We're missing some folks who said they might help us out this year," Wink said as he gazed around the rectangular conference table.

"Everyone is super busy with their own Christmas events, Wink," Eden said. "But a couple of people are still in phone and email contact with me. Even though they can't be here, they're gathering donated supplies and contacting possible vendors again to be sure they're on board."

"What else is left to do besides throw the party?" Frank asked. "Do we have everything we need?"

Eden looked down at the electronic tablet she used to keep track. "Plans are made, decorations are ordered, and Chief Ambrister and Berkley Metcalfe agreed to consult with the local Homeless Alliance to arrange transportation for our homeless vets both here in town and in Centerville to the facility."

"What vendors do we have confirmed?" Rachel asked.

Eden read the short list. "I'm hopeful for others who have yet to RSVP."

"If you'll email the list to me, I'll make those calls myself tomorrow."

"Thank you, Rachel, that would be a huge help."

Eden's salon was absolutely swamped this week and Mom had two doctor's appointments, one in Tulsa, for which Eden would have to carve out time. She was already staying up past midnight every night to juggle everything. And rising long before dawn.

The doorknob on the closed meeting room rattled. Eden stopped talking to wait for what she expected was a late-coming volunteer.

Instead, the door swung open and the bottom portion of a pair of crutches came into sight.

Eden's heart jumped. Adrenaline stung the back of her head.

She only knew one person on crutches.

In a split second, Rio Hendrix swung into the

room and scanned the faces as if on guard against imminent danger.

His gaze landed on her. "Sorry I'm late. Am I in the right place?"

She hoped so. From the bright smile on Taffy's face, so did she.

Brinkley, too, reacted, lifting his fuzzy head at the sound of Rio's voice.

"All volunteers are welcome, my boy. You being a veteran makes your attendance even more welcome." With lithe movement considering his age and diminutive size, Wink Myrick used his booted foot to shove an empty chair away from the table. "Have a seat. Eden was going over the updates."

"For those who don't know," Eden said, "this is Rio Hendrix, a friend of John-Parker Wisdom and Brandt James's." *And me.*

With a polite nod to the group, Rio settled to her left between Wink and Rachel, directly in Eden's line of vision. "She can catch me up later."

His comment brought speculative looks from the others in the group.

Ever the therapy dog, Brinkley rose and, tags jingling like Christmas bells, trotted over and lifted his paws onto Rio's knee. After an ear rub, the dog stretched his small form on the tiled floor next to Rio's chair and rested his chin on the boot cast.

Eden turned her attention back to the electronic tablet, though she was acutely aware that Rio was in the room.

Since sharing a car ride and burger two nights

ago, he'd called and texted several times. She'd replied to the texts with silly Christmas videos and, in turn, he'd sent hilarious dog memes, most of them involving harried groomers.

Who would believe from the dark, solemn look of him that the man had an enormous sense of humor?

Very appealing. Although now was not the time to think about Rio and his appeal.

Get it together, Eden. This is an important meeting. Focus on what's important.

Clearing her voice, she asked, "Ramona, have you heard back from the high school?"

"I have." Below a pixie haircut, the blond librarian's double row of ear studs sparkled when she moved. "The principal put me in contact with the senior class sponsor, Todd Gilkin. He's offered a group of seniors as servers and all-round help at the party. Says they are a great a group and they're eager to get involved in community service. College and job applications ask about that sort of thing."

"Perfect. Thank you. Now, for the most crucial part of the meeting." Worry tried to press in. Eden pushed back. "Sue do you have the treasurer's report?"

The middle-aged, perfectly coifed Sue Ann, slipped on a pair of reading glasses. "I do." A troubled look creased her brow. "I'm afraid it's not the news we were hoping for."

Sue Ann read the report and, with every word,

Eden's heart sank lower. Checking the faces of the other volunteers, she saw the disappointment in theirs, too.

Only Rio appeared nonplussed, one arm slung casually over the back of his chair, observing the proceedings with dispassionate, hooded eyes. But then, why should he care? He didn't even like Christmas. The cynic had probably only attended this meeting to give her a hard time about what he termed a bogus holiday.

As soon as the negative thought flashed into her head, Eden took it captive, refusing to believe the worst about anyone, especially a person who seemed as alone as Rio Hendrix. He'd been in her daily prayers and she chose to believe his appearance tonight was a good sign.

Taffy, who'd been ogling Rio since he'd entered the room, spoke up. "The party is Saturday after next. How can we possibly make enough money by then to pay for everything *and* to include the homeless veterans?"

"We'll have to leave them out again this year." Expression sad, Sue shook her head. "I'm sorry, Eden, truly, but I see no other solution. We just don't have the finances."

A masculine rumble interrupted. "What about a fundraiser?"

At his question, every head turned to stare at Rio.

Maybe he *had* come to offer help. Eden's heart expanded.

"Mom and I discussed that option already, but this group has been raising money all year." Rachel pushed a lock of brown hair behind one ear. "With the party date so soon, I don't see how we can put together another event in time."

Sue removed her readers and placed them on her notebook. "Then there's the problem of people being tapped out. We've hit all the donors in town. Plus, it *is* the holidays, after all, when most folks are stretched to the limit. Who would donate?"

"We can't give up." Eden heard the worry in her voice and modulated to hope. "Something will work out. We have to believe that. Now, instead of getting depressed, let's brainstorm ideas."

The upbeat comment was met with silence and apologetic expressions. Ann and Taffy shook their heads in resignation.

"Well, let's see." Frank scratched at his graying head. "The cheerleaders are selling candy. The student council is selling gift wrap. The Ag class is selling sausage. There's an Indian taco sale at the Community Church every Saturday. Too many sales, if you ask me, for us to try selling stuff."

"We don't have enough time to do sales anyway," Rachel said.

"And," Taffy added, "December is too cold to have another car wash."

The room grew silent again. They were right. Like the town, their group was small and everyone had lives of their own outside this one special event.

Time was short and a handful of people could only do so much.

But giving up was hard to do.

If it's God's will, it's God's bill, she reminded herself. Did that mean the inclusion of homeless veterans wasn't God's will?

Eden's energy faded along with the enthusiasm in the room.

Her long-held dream of including the homeless veterans died for lack of money.

All she could do now was focus on the positives.

After the meeting, the committee of despondent volunteers didn't stick around long and the room emptied quickly. Only Eden and the pixie blonde whom Rio had ascertained to be the librarian remained.

In no hurry to face the boredom of a hotel room and bothered by the disappointment he'd seen on Eden's normally happy face, Rio levered up on one foot, slid the crutches under his arms and hobbled around the conference table straightening chairs. He wanted to hang around to try to cheer her up.

The thought stopped him cold, made him smile. *Him* cheering *her*? That was a new one.

Brinkley left Rio in favor of his owner, a wise choice, all things considered. As if from habit, Eden let her fingertips graze the animal's head and, when he lifted his paws in a winsome plea for attention, she regained her smile.

It hadn't taken much for Mary Sunshine to reappear.

Maybe, if he was reassigned to another long-term operation, he'd get a dog. They were definitely mood lifters. Except the ones who'd broken his leg, and even they had turned out to be charmers. Yeah, a dog might be good.

If he was reassigned. *If* he didn't lose his job, his career, the only life he knew.

Half the time he still thought in Arabic instead of English. Yesterday, he'd almost inserted his dark brown contact lenses instead of the clear ones. And his suspicious nature had him checking the hotel room for spy bugs every time he returned.

If not for his Harley, he'd head back to Virginia the minute JP's wedding was over, though he'd be just as paranoid there, maybe more so. As part of his training and experience, he could blend in wherever he was, and small-town America was easy. He might not fit emotionally or intellectually, but he could slither into a crowd like a vapor without raising suspicions.

"Rio?"

He turned his focus to Eden. Had he surprised her by showing up here? Pleased her?

Their impromptu Mustang and burger "date," for lack of a better term, had him looking forward to her witty texts and thinking about her more than was prudent.

Yet, here he was.

"Thank you for coming." She cocked her head to

one side. Sincere and charming. Though serious, her brown eyes sparkled. "Does this mean you're on board to help with the Christmas party?"

Even if Christmas was bogus, the party would be enjoyed by his brothers-in-arms and remind them that they were not forgotten. So why not? He had nothing better to do with his time—such was the decision to which he'd arrived ten minutes before he'd hobbled through the library door.

"Let's put it this way. I'm all in for veterans. For any reason."

Eden offered him a dazzling laser of a smile, complete with mile-deep dimples that wiped his mental hard drive.

"Me, too!" She pumped one arm. "Vets 'R' Us! The party is so much fun. You're going to love it."

Love might be taking things a bit far.

"Too bad about the finances." In his view, every veteran, regardless of dwelling place, deserved honor. Homeless vets were often the most forgotten and Eden's desire to include them touched a chord in him.

"Everything will work out." Optimism back in place, Eden slid her iPad into a tote emblazoned with a canine-imprinted ad for Eden's Dog Grooming Salon. "If not this year, then next."

"I might have an idea." Brought on by her and her tote bag.

Eden's brown eyes lit up. "Tell me. At this point, I am so out of ideas."

Rio nudged his chin toward the door. The pixie

blonde had peeked inside twice already. Ever watchful, he'd noticed the other woman's presence even if Eden hadn't. "Your librarian is waiting to lock up."

"Oh, right." Going to the exit, with him lurching along behind on one foot and two crutches, Eden called out, "Sorry, Ramona. You can lock up now. I'm leaving. Thank you."

"No problem." But the blonde came toward them with a wad of keys in one hand.

Holding the exit door with his shoulder, Rio waited while Eden and Brinkley walked through.

The door swooshed closed behind them. Rio heard the keys rattle, a reminder that the librarian was there alone.

He paused. The world was a dangerous place and he doubted Ramona knew a dozen ways to neutralize a threat. He did. Even with crutches.

"We should wait," he said.

"I was thinking the same thing."

After the librarian locked up, they walked her to her car and said their goodbyes. Brinkley trotted along with them. The jingle of his tags blended with the tap of footsteps on pavement. The town had grown quiet and only an occasional vehicle motored down the adjacent street.

"Now, what's this idea you have?" Eden shifted the tote bag on her arm.

"Let me carry that."

"I've got it." For emphasis, her eyes, shiny even

in the dim light, raked over his crutches. "What's your idea?"

"Too cold to talk outside. Meet me at the coffee shop."

With a tweet of the remote, Eden unlocked her car and slid inside. Gilded by the golden security light, her pretty face turned up toward him.

"How about Braum's Ice Cream Shop instead? They have both coffee and ice cream. Burgers, chicken strips and salads, too, if you're hungry." She offered him a peek at her dimples.

He had the most bizarre desire to lean forward and kiss her sweet smile. "Ice cream it is."

"Don't rush," she said, "I'll be a minute. I have to drop Brinkley at home and check on Grandpa first."

Using the top of her door for balance, Rio shifted his crutches so that he was closer. The interior of her car smelled like coconut. In the passenger seat, Brinkley waited next to a dog harness attached to the seat belt. Smart dog.

Out of habit, Rio scanned the back seat. All clear. Safe. "Want me to follow and pick you up in the Mustang?"

"No need. I'll meet you at Braum's in about fifteen minutes. Okay?"

Not really. "Sounds good."

Before he could do something entirely out of character, Rio closed her door, swung his crutches as quickly as he could move away from temptation, and headed for his car.

***

Neither Rio nor his muscle car were anywhere in sight when Eden entered the ever-busy ice cream shop. Finding an open booth next to the huge picture windows, she slid onto the hard plastic seat to wait. Some of the customers were familiar, so she alternately waved and smiled to those who caught her eye. A couple who frequented her grooming services for their Great Pyrenees stopped by the booth, double-decker waffle cones in hand, to chat.

Rosemary Ridge was that kind of town; one of the reasons she loved living there. This time of year, she loved the area even more. As in most businesses, garland, tinsel and bright red bows festooned the building. Even the employees got into the fun with red aprons and Santa hats or headbands like the ones she'd given Rio.

She wondered what he'd done with them.

After a ten-minute wait, she texted him. Are you lost?

The instant she sent the message, Rio and his crutches swung through the automated door.

Pausing, he scanned the room, although she was certain he'd already spotted her, and then made his way to the booth.

"Ignore the text message I sent just now."

Instead, he yanked out his cell phone and read the screen.

"You missed me." He flashed a teasing smirk. "Did you think I'd stand you up?"

Eden's belly fluttered. That's exactly what she'd

thought. And now his flirty response had her questioning her motives. Had she agreed to meet him because of the party? Or because she liked being with him?

Probably both. *And,* she told herself firmly, *there is nothing wrong with enjoying the man's company and making him feel welcome.* Especially since she'd been the cause of the injury keeping him in town. He was also a veteran. A hero, in her opinion.

She motioned toward the booth seat opposite hers. "I didn't want to miss out on this idea of yours."

"Heartbreaker," he accused.

Eden knew he teased, but his eyes looked serious.

After pushing the crutches to the inside of the opposite seat and out of the way of other customers, Rio slid in next to them.

"Tell me this idea," Eden said. "I'm desperate."

He held up in an index finger. "Ice cream first. Talk second."

"You're torturing me."

"Sort of like the videos you force me to watch?" His chuckle slid over her skin, warm and masculine. "What would you like?"

"To know your idea."

"Tsk, tsk. So impatient. Ice cream, Eden. Ice cream. Banana split? Triple sundae with hot fudge?" He squinted toward the menu board. "Eggnog, gingerbread or peppermint ice cream cone?"

Eden aimed a pointed look toward the crutches. "I'll get the order. What will you have?"

With a beleaguered sigh as though she'd taken away his man card, he told her and she went to the register to order, returning in a few minutes with a tray of sundaes.

"Yours looks amazing," she said about his Black Forest sundae, a mix of chocolate cake and ice cream drizzled with hot fudge and cherry topping. The man liked his chocolate.

He reached for her spoon, scooped into the concoction and offered it to her. "Try a bite."

She took the bite and hummed appreciation of the intense flavor before scooting her bowl toward him. "Try mine. Hot caramel over butter pecan ice cream with salted pecans and whipped cream. I went for the protein." And then she laughed.

Rio tried hers then dipped into the cherry topping on his. "I'm all about the fruit. Healthy."

"Who knew this was a health food store? I have to come here more often."

They dug into their sundaes and were silent for a couple of minutes. As the combo of cold ice cream and hot, salty caramel tantalized her tongue, Eden relaxed, comfortable in Rio's company in a way that surprised her considering the short time of their acquaintance.

He was an enigma, but she liked him. Never mind his good looks, he intrigued her and fueled her desire to eradicate the darkness that clung to him. But for all his mystery, he made her laugh, too.

Complicated. That was the best word to describe Rio Hendrix.

He'd been a foster child. He'd also served in the Rangers, seen danger, faced battle. Were those the reasons for the aura of sadness? The heaviness in his spirit? The negative energy?

Long, tanned fingers nudged her plastic sundae dish. "You're too quiet. Scares me."

"I'm thinking." About him. But she wouldn't admit that. "Are you going to keep me in suspense all night or tell me your wonderful idea?"

"I don't know how wonderful it is. You may have already done something of this nature, or, since it involves you donating your time and dog salon, you may not approve or have time."

She was swamped, both inside the salon and outside, but if the idea proved lucrative enough, she'd make time. Somehow. "Tell me."

He contemplated the end of his empty plastic spoon. "What if you, with help from your volunteers, including me and anyone else we can arm-twist, put on a one-day dog spa extravaganza?"

Eden furrowed her brow. "I don't think that would bring in enough money."

He stopped her protest with a raised hand. "Hear me out."

"Okay." She took a bite of ice cream, letting it melt on her tongue as she listened.

"Not just dog baths and haircuts, but get others involved. Rally local services to donate their talents that day."

She still didn't see where he was going with this. But he was brilliant and worth a listen. "Such as?"

"Think big. For instance, isn't your friend Taffy a photographer?"

"Oh." The light came on. "I see what you're saying. Taffy might be willing to take photos with owners and their freshly groomed pets. People love that and would pay for them."

And *she* loved Rio's idea and appreciated him for trying to help. Had God sent him along to make things work out for her good and the good of her veterans?

The thought almost made her laugh. She knew God often used the least likely to do His will. Was he using Rio right now? And what would Rio think if she told him so?

"Photos are only the beginning, Eden. On the way over, I brainstormed a few other ideas." He pushed aside his half-eaten sundae and whipped out his cell phone. "Rosemary Ridge has some other dog-related businesses. The veterinarian and the pet store are two examples."

Excitement started to bubble inside Eden. Rio was right. She'd been stuck in a single mindset of doing most of the work herself with only a handful of friends. But if they spread their outreach to include more businesses, they just might have a chance.

"Rachel Colter is one of our volunteers and she's the veterinarian's wife," she told him. "Her husband, Jake, is a great guy. I'm confident he'd donate some checkups or talk to owners about health care for pets or *something* veterinarian-ish that could generate donations."

The corners of his lips lifted at her invented word. "What about the pet store? Know anyone there?"

"Probably. I'll give them a call tomorrow. See if they'll donate some items for sale. People buy their pets gifts at Christmas." She took out her cell phone and jotted the ideas in the notes section. "I'll call Rachel and Taffy, too. We'll have to work fast to make this happen."

"JP and Brandt know people. I'll contact them first thing in the morning." He glanced at his phone list again. "Know anyone who can bake? Or put on a mini obedience clinic? Except you. You're the groomer."

"Lots of people can bake. Are we having a bake sale, too?"

"That's actually a good idea I hadn't considered. Food while they shop and groom. Jot that down, but I'm also thinking dog treats. Donated homemade, healthy dog treats for sale. Stocking stuffers for the pups."

"Brilliant idea!" Ice cream temporarily forgotten, Eden clapped her hands in a soundless staccato and gave a silent squeal. This could work. This could actually work! "Since the high school kids want to do community service, some of them could be our bakers."

"What about JP and Zoey's teenagers? Zoey's a superb cook."

"Yes. Yes! Perfect. Customers would receive something they actually want in exchange for their hard-earned money." Unlike another plea-for-donations drive. "We'll call it a *bark*ery!"

Energy sparking like fireworks, Eden figured she'd be up all night tonight working on this one last fundraiser. But she didn't care. If God was making a way, she'd jump in and do her part.

"If we work quickly, we can make this happen, Rio." She reached across the table and clutched his hand. "You're a genius."

Actually, he was, if she remembered correctly.

"Sometimes a fresh perspective is all you need." His serious gaze connected with hers. He rotated his hands so their fingers laced together. "I'm glad to be useful."

His warm, strong contact shot another bolus of energy into Eden's bloodstream.

She offered him a smile and watched his eyes light up, as if making her happy made him happy, too.

A woman could fall for a man like that.

Chapter Eight

Rio's idea seemed to ignite the Veterans Christmas Committee with fresh intent. With emails and texts flying, they divided duties and set to work. By the end of the first day, Eden jumped on a video call with all of them to report that every single local business they'd contacted had agreed to take part. While their roles in the event were still to be finalized, they were on board with donating their resources in some way. And Eden could think of plenty of ways they could help!

Unsurprisingly, Rio was a computer whiz who created memes and ads and emailed them to every volunteer with instructions to flood social media. With a nudge from photographer Taffy, he even convinced Eden to star with Brinkley in a charming dog video for uploading. And if that wasn't enough, he drove to the veterans' home to film brief stories with his smartphone of three of the men who'd agreed to have them posted online.

Meanwhile, Taffy wrangled a free half-page announcement from the local newspaper and the one in Centerville in exchange for photos and a write-up of the event. KEBH Radio in Centerville began publicizing the event every hour for the next three days, another coup she credited to Rio. He called their efforts a media blitz, and he was good at it, generating a new idea as fast as Eden could keep up.

The man seemed to be good at everything. If a need arose, Rio was on it, and he seemed as energized as she was by the late nights working together and the progress each day brought.

If she wasn't careful, Eden mused, she might get a crush on the former high school heartthrob. Maybe she already had.

From the way he looked at her and occasionally touched her elbow or her shoulder, she thought he could be feeling the same attraction to her. This, of course, would not do. Rio was not only anxious to return to his mysterious government job, he wasn't a believer, and that was a nonstarter in Eden's book.

They could, however, be friendly teammates. Right now she needed him and was convinced God had sent him to work all things for the ultimate good of her and a whole lot of veterans. Maybe, just maybe, to make things better for him, too.

Acts of kindness worked in both directions.

By the next Saturday morning at five o'clock, weary but excited, Eden dressed in a Christmas smock, slipped on her Santa hat and opened the salon, welcoming the volunteers and vendors, both inside and outside her small building with hats and headbands of their own.

Before going inside the shop, she quickly surveyed the wide space between the salon and Grandpa's back door, grinning at the Christmas lights strung along the fences and around the tables. Rio had groaned yesterday when she'd insisted on the lights, the red bows and her old boom box to play Christmas carols. But even as he'd glowered, he'd helped volunteers with the decorations.

He was coming along. If she had her way, he'd be celebrating Christmas right along with her by Christmas Day.

Somehow during the last few days and late nights, Rio and the Myrick brothers had squeezed in time to erect makeshift pens to cordon off various activities. A petting zoo, a dog adoptionpen, and an obedience trainer had set up shop in separate areas, taking donations in exchange for services and "free" puppies or dogs, all of them with neutering vouchers from Drs. Colter and Howell. Even the pet store had put up an outdoor booth with various pet goods to sell, including Christmas sweaters, blankets and reindeer hats.

Wink and Frank Myrick were working the welcome table, signing in customers to rotate through their areas of interest, and gleefully raking in the resulting cash. Delighted by their bright red shirts, Eden perched a Santa hat on Frank's head. Wink took a pair of reindeer antlers and jammed them atop his cowboy hat.

To the Myricks' left, their brother Catfish, an accomplished chef and baker, manned a white-clothed table of his fancy cookies and cakes along with other donated bake sale items. Eden's grandpa, oxygen pack at his side, joined the rotund Catfish to welcome the growing crowd as friendly ambassadors.

The result was organized chaos accented with laughter, calls of "Merry Christmas" and a festive community atmosphere that spilled over to the inner salon.

During another late hour the night before, Eden and Rio had reorganized the interior salon to make more room. Three stations allowed volunteers to brush, shampoo and dry the dogs—with her guidance, of course. In assembly-line form, with laughter and splashes, they rotated their canine customers through the stations while the two veterinarians gave checkups and vaccinations and waiting dog owners browsed the options out on the lawn.

Eden was elbow-deep in suds assisting with a squirmy hound when Rio came through the door accompanied by two men she recognized from the veterans' home, Hank and Ronnie. Each proudly wore a military cap announcing his branch of service.

But the man who captured her attention was the one on crutches. She hadn't seen him yet this morning and, after spending every spare minute in his company for the past few days, she'd missed him—even though he'd been there until three this morning working on last-minute preparations.

Their gazes collided. Held.

He looked...great. Rested, as if he'd had ten full

hours every night this week instead of three or four. More than great. He looked pleased, as if working himself into exhaustion had erased some of his heaviness.

Eden doubted she looked half as good. Eye drops hadn't erased all the redness from her eyes, but after seeing this crowd, her energy buzzed and she felt like a million dollars whether she looked good or not.

Staring at Rio made the buzz stronger.

Time to stop staring and get on with business.

Shaking off the suds, she turned the squirmy hound over to two volunteers and went to greet the veterans, drying her hands on her apron as she moved through the crowded room.

"I wondered if you'd stood me up again." She flashed Rio a smile to let him know she joked.

One of the older veterans glared at Rio. "You better treat her right, sonny boy."

Rio's teeth gleamed white against his dark tan. "She's only giving me a hard time, Hank. I would never stand this lady up." His eyes captured hers again as if he, too, had a hard time controlling his gazes this morning. "Ever."

Eden experienced a flutter beneath her rib cage. Going without breakfast would do that to her. And she was overexcited. She wanted to blame her reactions on what was starting out to be a successful event, but she couldn't. The blame lay squarely on herself and the man with the secret blue eyes.

"Isn't this amazing?" She swept a hand around

the room and toward the outside. "Customers were already lining the lawn before we opened."

"Impressive," he said with a gleam of satisfaction. "And the day is young. My men and I have more to add."

The man's brain never slowed down. Eden loved that about him. Rather, she liked it. Liked, not loved.

She patted her heated cheeks.

Noting the poster board in Hank's hands, she refocused there. "What is this, Hank?"

"The guys at the home put together a display," Ronnie said. "You do so much for us. We want to do our part. Show folks what they're contributing to."

"And join the fun." Hank opened the folded board to display a collection of photos. "See how handsome I was?" He elbowed Rio. "Rio, my boy, back in the day, I woulda give you a run for your money for this little gal."

The heat of a flattered blush rose on the back of Eden's neck. Again. She must be overly tired to let herself react this way to everything related to Rio Hendrix.

"You looked amazing in your dress whites, Hank. These photos are wonderful. Which one is you, Ronnie?" She held up a hand, stop-sign style. "Wait, don't tell me. Let me find you."

She searched the photos, so aware of Rio standing close that she had trouble concentrating.

When was the last time she'd felt this alive in a man's presence?

As in *never!*

She really *was* getting a crush. Infatuation with a smart, good-looking man who exuded mystery. Any woman would be interested, wouldn't she?

"There!" In a desperate attempt to stop the flow of gushy thoughts, Eden poked a finger at a slender soldier in fatigues with a green helmet in hand. "I'd recognize that mischievous grin anywhere."

Ronnie chortled. "That's me, all right, before I shipped out to Germany. You know these other fellas, too. All of them from the facility."

A lump thickened Eden's throat. The old men she visited at the veterans' home had once been young, their whole lives in front of them. Most, like Grandpa when he'd shipped out to Vietnam, had only been teenage boys. They'd sacrificed years of their young lives for the greater good so that people like her could live in peace and freedom.

The reminder made her even more determined to make this Celebrate Veterans Christmas Party the best one ever.

"This is fabulous, Ronnie. Hank. We'll set the board up—" she glanced around the tight space "—somewhere."

"We got this." Rio took the board from her, his fingers brushing hers. Had they lingered just a little too long? "I just spoke by phone with JP. His boys and Zoey are on their way with more homemade dog treats. Hank and Ronnie are manning the sales with them."

"Perfect." Both the older gents were outgoing

and mentally sharp. Hank had been an accountant after his naval service. Who better to handle sales?

Her glance flicked to the man who'd thought to include them today. Flutters danced in her stomach.

"Miss Zoey brought the boys over to Centerville yesterday," Ronnie was saying, "and us vets packaged treats in little cellophane bags. Chief Warrant Officer Hendrix made some fancy-looking labels for them on that computer, and here we are! Ready to do our part."

Chief Warrant Officer Hendrix. Eden hadn't known that about Rio. But she saw the respect the men had for him, and he clearly returned the feeling.

Who would have expected a hard-eyed Scrooge who claimed not to like Christmas and who was ambivalent about God to have such a tender heart?

Yes, she was getting a serious crush.

"You guys are fantastic. No wonder I love you all." She gave the older gents each a side hug.

"Well, now," Hank sputtered, his cheeks turning pink. "We're fond of you, too, little miss."

"Eden," someone called from behind her. "We need your help."

Eden pivoted sideways toward the grooming stations to see a volunteer waving her over.

"Sorry, guys," she said. "Duty calls."

Rio touched her elbow, fingertips light and easy, though they sent a charge through her body. Did he feel it? Or was the giant dose of electricity her imagination? And infatuation?

Definitely getting a crush.

"Go." His quiet baritone rumbled through her, activating more electricity that raised the hairs on the back of her neck. In a good way. "I'll get the others set up and see how things are going outside."

"Report back?"

His nostrils flared, and in a tone as serious as if he'd received orders to storm the beaches of Normandy, he answered, "You got it."

What was he doing here, knee-deep in a Christmas fundraiser of all things, among normal, everyday citizens of small-town America?

Rio asked himself that question for the tenth time as he moved among the tables and the outdoor stations. *Moved* was too strong a word. His leg was broken. He barely hobbled around on those frustrating crutches.

He needed to get back to Virginia and then halfway across the world to an assignment. He needed to know the US government still saw him as a valuable asset in the ongoing war on terror. And he needed his physically fit, vigorous body back in prime op mode.

Yet here he was. Useless, in small town America, surrounded by more Christmas than he'd experienced in years.

What had gotten into him?

But he knew. It wasn't a question of *what*. It was a question of *who*.

That bright little elf—Eden the effervescent

one—with her dogs and friends and Christmas cheer had sucked him in like a multi-vortex tornado.

At first, he'd blamed boredom for his involvement in her op, but something had shifted these past few days of constant contact, of watching and interacting with her. He liked Eden Carnegie. *Really* liked her.

This, in itself, did not pose a problem. He liked women in general and usually found female companionship wherever he went, even during an op. The longer the op, the longer the girlfriend lasted. The problem was his job. Those relationships—in fact every relationship he'd had—were, because of his work, shallow. Empty.

None of those women had known who he really was. They hadn't even known his real name, much less that he worked intelligence for the US government, and that he'd use any information he could gain from their relationship to further his mission. It was the job. It was what he did, who he was, fighting for the moral good. Freedom was his cause and he felt no guilt in using whoever and whatever he could to achieve that end.

The situation with Eden, however, was different. Very different. She was open and honest, kind to a fault. Warm as sunshine. Light to his darkness.

He'd never known anyone quite like her. He had nothing to gain from their friendship, but because of Eden, he'd spent the past week doing something completely unnatural. Party planning. Fundraising. For Christmas, of all the bogus events.

His eyes landed on the old men stationed around the yard. Hank, Ronnie, Eden's grandpa. Even the Myrick brothers. All of them veterans. Men who'd served this nation the same as him. This fundraiser and his involvement were for them. Mostly.

If not for the effervescent one, he would have maintained his distance.

She even had him thinking about God. Her God, who seemed very different from the other gods he'd encountered across the world. A god Eden claimed was like a good loving father who wanted the best for her.

Rio huffed. Intriguing, but a figment of her Pollyanna imagination.

Not that he would know anything about a good father.

Was Eden's Jesus the reason for her positive attitude even in the setbacks? She hadn't pushed her religion at him but she had lived it in front of him, dropping a hint here and there of God's goodness to her. Courtesy of the overdose of Christmas décor and "Silent Night" wafting from the boom box, this Jesus thing had suddenly invaded his thoughts. Because of Eden.

He looked down at his booted foot and almost laughed. He could credit Eden with that, too, though his unbroken leg gave him more trouble than the broken one. After a week of limping about, erecting wire fences, moving furniture and setting up tables, his good leg ached all the way up his back.

He was getting old.

Checking with each vendor as he hobbled across the dry grass, Rio paused at the puppy pen. At least a dozen pups of all shapes, sizes and colors tumbled over each other and the visitors. Two children seated on the ground giggled in delight as joyful puppies swarmed them.

Though the mid-December air seeped through Rio's layered shirts and chilled his skin, the happy sight warmed the inside of his chest. Kids and puppies; they seemed to go together in innocent joy unaware that they were surrounded by evil.

Not that he'd ever owned an animal, so what did he know?

He watched for a few minutes until the ache in his back increased. He could ignore the pain, but why bother when he could rest instead? No one seemed to need him right now. The area appeared to be humming along as planned. Safe. Not a suspicious person in sight.

Swinging his crutches through the buzzing crowd of cheery shoppers, he found an empty chair at the Myrick brothers' table next to Eden's grandpa.

"Take a load off, son," Frank said.

That's exactly what he needed to do.

"Thanks." He also needed to report back to Eden. An excuse, he knew, but he'd promised. "Just for a minute."

"What's the rush? Things seem to be running like clockwork," Wink said.

"I have orders from the colonel to run surveillance and report back to her." He'd take her one of those barbecue sandwiches, too. The scent of smoked meat, courtesy of the fire department, made his mouth water.

The three older gents chuckled.

"Got you running, does she? Or maybe I should say hobblin'?" Ronnie slapped his leg and laughed.

Rio smiled at the corny joke. "For a good cause. Glad to help."

"That girl's got irons in so many fires, I don't know how she keeps up," Hank says, "especially with her personal problems."

"She never seems to have a bad day." Even when things weren't going her way and the discussion turned serious, the light never left Eden's face. She could always smile and flash those charming dimples.

How did she do that?

"That's my Eden," her grandpa, Steven, said. "Focuses on the bright side. For years, she's been looking after me and her mama without a complaint. Claims it's a privilege because she loves us." Steven harrumphed, gray head shaking. "She fought like a tiger to keep her mama at home as long as she could."

Rio frowned. "What happened to her mother?"

"Alzheimer's. Mean disease. After Eden's dad was killed, Eden and Helen moved in with me.

You probably knew that." The older man paused for a few draws on his oxygen, barrel chest rising and falling in short puffs. "We needed each other, you see, during those awful grieving years. I was happy to have them to look after, but as I've aged and her mama got sick, the burden of looking after each other fell more and more to Eden alone."

"I didn't know about her mom." Rio vaguely recalled that Eden's dad had died in the Middle East, and she'd lived her childhood with her grandfather the cop. The rest was news. "Eden's optimism had me thinking she'd never faced any hardships."

"Oh, she's had plenty of those." Steven leaned back against the chair for a minute and deep-breathed from the oxygen tubes.

"Don't we all?" Wink put in.

His brother nudged him with an elbow. "Most of us don't keep on smiling the way Eden does. You can be a grump. So can I."

"If you had dimples that cute, you'd smile more, too."

Frank guffawed and rubbed one cheek. "Wouldn't I look a sight with big old holes in my cheeks?"

The old men chuckled as a couple with three children approached the table for directions to the puppies.

After they'd signed in, with a reminder from Hank to stop back with a donation, they moved on. The kids' laughter carried back to Rio's ears. Kids. Puppies. Christmas. He was definitely out of his element.

Rio pondered the revelations about the effervescent one. All this time, he'd misjudged Eden because of her big smile and positive attitude.

Now, he knew the truth.

His respect, admiration and, if he'd admit it, his attraction to Eden Carnegie shot up and tumbled off the charts.

Chapter Nine

At nine o'clock that night, the crowd had thinned and Eden finished one last grooming customer on her own. Exhausted volunteers filed out to the lawn to take down tables and folding chairs to return to the church before tomorrow.

Taffy, whose camera hadn't stopped all day, waited in the Christmas-decorated photo booth to snap one last Christmas card photo. This one of Dr. Colter and Rachel with their children, Daley and baby Matthew, and their charming Irish setter, Moose.

Eden finished brushing Moose's now-shiny red fur and let him hop to the floor. "How does he look?"

Rachel, seated against the only vacant wall, baby Matthew in her arms, smiled. "If only he'd stay this clean. He's beautiful after you groom him."

"He's a handsome animal," Eden said, "but it's Moose's personality that makes him a winner. I love whenever he comes to visit. Such a charmer."

Moose, obviously aware that he was the center of admiration, shook himself, tail wagging as he shot Eden a doggy smile and then trotted to the little girl.

Brinkley rose from his sleigh bed and came over to say hello to his friend. The two touched noses before Brinkley returned to his bed with a sigh. Today had been a long day for him, too, even though Grandpa had taken him outside twice to visit. Like her, Brinkley enjoyed company, but he was tired.

Daley only had eyes for Moose. "Sit, Moosey. Sit."

The six-year-old swirled a fur-lined Santa cape over the dog's back and slipped a set of brown reindeer antlers over his head. Moose looked ridiculously cute.

"Now for the pictures, Mommy." Daley spun in a circle, showing off her holiday outfit. "I didn't get dirty, either, when you let me pet the puppies. See?"

"Ready when you are," Taffy called from her booth.

After Rachel adjusted Daley's lopsided hair bow, the family moved to the Christmas backdrop.

Hands on her hips, pleased with today, Eden slowly surveyed the salon. The place was a mess, though volunteers had tried to keep the floor dry and the used towels in the bin. Supplies scattered over the surfaces, makeshift stations needed to be sanitized and stored, a pile of brushes and other grooming tools waited in the main sink to be cleaned. The washer/dryer needed to be filled and run.

So much left to do.

She rotated her head and heard the crack of tired neck muscles. "Might as well get busy."

As she began cleaning the salon and putting away supplies, Eden wondered if they'd reached their financial goal. No matter how busy they'd been—and they'd been delightfully slammed all day—the verdict came down to how much people were willing and able to donate for the services provided.

She was cautiously hopeful.

The door opened and Rio swung inside. Regardless of her fatigue, Eden's pulse jumped and shot a charge of fresh energy through her veins.

"The lawn has been evacuated. Perimeter is secure," he said with an almost-grin.

"Did you leave the lights up and on?"

"No décor was harmed during this mission. Nor were any animals or humans. 'Feliz Navidad' reigns supreme in the Carnegie yard."

Eden laughed. She loved when he teased. Even though he didn't smile a lot, his humor popped up often. A good sign that he was more than his dark countenance.

What had happened in his past to fuel such cynicism?

"Any report yet on how much money we raised?"

He lifted a trio of bank bags. "We'll soon know."

"How does it look?"

"Good, I think, if my mental calculations serve. Want to count the money now?"

A thrill bubbled through Eden's fatigue. Given his mental abilities, she had high expectation that his calculations were correct.

"Yes, I would, but the salon—" She waved a weary hand around the space.

"Leave it. We'll clean in the morning."

That meant he was willing to help. Again. "Can't. Church."

His eyes shuttered. "Oh, yeah."

Eden noticed the subtle change but casually asked anyway, "Want to go with me? Ten thirty?"

"I'll clean the salon."

She was disappointed, though she'd expected the response. He closed down anytime she talked about her faith. "Thanks, but let's leave this until afternoon."

There was more to cleaning the salon than putting supplies back on shelves. He wouldn't know that, of course and, deep down, she was glad for an excuse to spend the afternoon in his company.

"Your call." He pivoted on one foot toward the photo booth. The Colters were about to leave. Dr. Colter pulled out his wallet.

Eden waved him off. "Oh, no, you don't, Dr. Colter. You and Rachel have given so much already to make this successful. How many vaccines and checkups did you donate today? At least thirty, I know. Not counting the vouchers you handed out."

"Forty-two but that's not important." He plunked a large bill onto a table. "What you've done here is not only good for the veterans, it's good for the community. I'm happy to take part."

She shook her head, holding back a sudden surge of grateful tears. Fatigue was getting the best of her. "I don't even know what to say, except thank you. And Moose gets free grooming for the rest of his life."

Rachel laughed as Daley hung on to Moose's neck with adoration. "Be careful what you promise. This boy loves a mud puddle."

"I mean it. Bring him anytime. He and I are pals." She rubbed Moose's ears and received a doggy smile in return.

Affection welled in her. These dogs, loving and innocent, filled an empty spot in her life. While she waited—and prayed—for the other fulfillment she longed for.

The family left and, with them, Eden's secret wish for a family of her own. Rachel had waited for many years before she and the animal doctor remarried, so perhaps there was still hope for Eden.

Brinkley, the sweetheart, must have felt her yearning because, as he always did whenever a longing settled over her, he trotted to her side. She picked him up for a nuzzle, enjoying the warmth and affection he shared so easily.

Emotion rose in her throat. She was exhausted. That's all. If God wanted her to have a family, He'd give her one. She trusted Him.

Lowering Brinkley to the floor, she helped Taffy gather her equipment and props, and with assistance from Rio, loaded them in Taffy's VW Bug. The one with the sunflower painted on the side.

The sunshiny reminder put a spark back in Eden's mood. Today had been fantastic. She was blessed. Life was wonderful. Christmas was the best! No matter what the proceeds of today, they would ensure her veterans had the brightest, merriest Christmas possible.

As the VW's red taillights disappeared down the street, the Carnegie yard, so joyfully noisy all day, grew quiet and dark except for the array of Christmas lights chasing each other along the fence tops and around the door of her salon.

Brinkley, delighted to be off-leash at last, raced around the lawn sniffing the dog pens. He was probably looking for a familiar friend.

"I have to believe we made our goal," she murmured. "In fact, I feel very positive."

Rio snorted. "Since when did you feel anything else?"

Oh, about five minutes ago, she thought but smiled instead. "Dr. Colter's right. Even if we don't have enough to include all the homeless veterans, we can include some. And we've done a wonderful thing, Rio. Lots of wonderful things. People came together for a common cause and celebrated the holiday at the same time. People enjoyed their neighbors and received some incredibly valuable services. Shelter dogs found homes. Families spent time together."

"Family is important to you, isn't it?"

Something in his voice turned her head to gaze at him. In the shadowy light, he looked pensive.

"Very important. I wish my family was bigger, but I have Mom and Grandpa, and they mean the world to me."

"Steven told me about your mother. I'm sorry."

Ah, so that was why he'd mentioned family.

They should go back inside, but she liked being here in the dim light with Rio, the festive ambience reminding her of all the positive things they'd accomplished today.

"I'm sorry, too," she said, "And I pray for a miracle every morning and night."

He shifted on his crutches. "How's that working out for you?"

Eden crossed her arms against the deepening chill of the night and maybe against the cynicism in Rio's voice.

"Mom still knows who I am. That's huge. We have good days together. Most of all, she's still on this planet with me. Those are answers to prayer, so I'm encouraged. I know God looks after my best interests and Mom's, too."

He remained silent, but she felt his stare against her skin.

After a moment, he and his crutches moved closer.

Deep baritone soft, he murmured, "You're a special woman, Eden Carnegie."

Something in his voice sifted over her, warm and comforting. Though Eden tried to keep her reply light, the words came out in a whisper. "You're pretty special yourself, Rio Hendrix."

"Yeah." As if she'd offended him, he started to turn away.

Eden caught his upper arm. "Rio?"

He paused but didn't turn back. Some emotion she didn't understand throbbed from him. The atmosphere trembled with tension.

"I should go," he said. "You're tired."

Puzzled by the sudden change, she asked, "Did I do something wrong?"

He turned then to pierce the darkness with those intense blue eyes of his. "You? No. Never you."

"What then?"

She heard the deep, deep breath he inhaled before he answered. "I wish I could tell you."

"You can tell me anything, Rio, and trust it stays in here." She patted the spot over her heart.

With a hint of a sad smile, he said, "I believe you. But I like you far too much."

Cryptic comment simmering in the darkness, Rio swiveled on his crutches and headed toward the dog salon.

Brinkley broke away from his job as chief sniffer to catch up. His dog tags jingled against the quiet.

Bewildered, Eden followed the pair. Rio held the door open for her and Brinkley to enter first. A perfect gentleman. Respectful. A man who cared about other people. For the veterans. For her. A good man but an enigma.

On the exterior, he was strong and confident, a

take-charge-and-do-things-right warrior for honor and good.

But in this moment, he seemed utterly alone.

And Eden's heart ached for him.

Rio stumbled up the steps into the salon. He'd wanted to tell Eden about his own terribly fractured family. Maybe he'd also wanted to tell her about the other, something he'd never been tempted to do before.

Not one woman in his life, aside from his mother, had ever affected him this strongly.

He *trusted* her. Now *that* was a wild admission for a man who'd been trained to trust no one but himself.

He must be losing his grip. At best, fatigue was messing with his head.

Taking the money bags from the small desk jammed into one corner of the salon, he dragged a folding chair over and began to count the proceeds from the day. Anything to get his mind off his bizarre reaction in the dark yard.

Brinkley raised both paws onto Rio's knee. A therapy dog, Eden claimed. The small animal seemed to feel his mood. Rio lifted him onto his lap. Brinkley rewarded him with a cold nose against his neck. In spite of his troubled thoughts, Rio's mouth curved. He ruffled the shaggy fur.

Another folding chair clanked next to his. Eden extended a candy cane beneath his nose.

As if he hadn't acted at all strange a few minutes ago, she said, "How are we doing?"

Taking the peppermint candy, he shot her a sideglance. "Personally or economically?"

Instead of the flash of dimples he expected, she offered a solemn gaze. "Both. Are you okay?"

"Yes." As if Brinkley recognized the lie, the little dog placed both paws on his chest and licked his cheek.

Eden laughed. "Brinkley, stop. Get down."

She started to reach for the dog, but Rio said, "Leave him. He's my buddy."

"If he annoys you, put him on the floor."

"He won't." He handed her a pile of money. "Sort into denominations. We don't have a lot of change. I'll count that."

Eden's expression said she knew he'd purposely focused the topic away from himself and onto the money, but she nodded and took the bills.

With only the noise of cellophane crinkling from the candy canes, a few wiggles from Brinkley and the click of stacked coins, they spent the next minutes counting and recounting the funds.

Rio poked one end of the candy cane in the corner of his mouth and gnawed as he counted. From the corner of his eye, he saw Eden do the same. She still wore a Christmas smock and her Santa hat. Had he ever seen her without the hat?

As the count dwindled, Rio's neck muscles tightened. He wanted this event to be a success for the veterans. But mostly to make Eden happy.

She'd gotten under his skin, something he never allowed in the field. Ever.

Good thing his time in Rosemary Ridge was limited. If he wasn't careful, she'd have him spilling state secrets and crying on her shoulder. Something else he had never—and would never—do. What he did and what he knew was much more important than his feelings.

But he could enjoy the limited time he and Eden had together. Like he did with other women.

Except she wasn't any other woman.

When the last bill was counted and entered into the calculator, Eden turned her pretty face to him. The brightest smile he'd ever seen deepened her dimples.

"We did it, Rio."

"You did it."

She shook her head. "Without your idea, I'd still be praying for answers."

"I'm not answered prayer."

"Oh, I think you are." She reached for Brinkley, placed him on the ground, leaned in and gave him an awkward hug. "Thank you. I'm so excited."

So was he, though he didn't show it. The awkward hug had shot through him like a bullet. He wanted to rearrange himself and try again, this time for a full-on embrace.

He glanced at his cell phone. "It's late. You have church."

"I'll be up half the night celebrating. Who can sleep now?"

"I can sleep anytime, anywhere." A necessary skill he'd developed in the rangers. His only sleepless nights were when he tried to contact his dad. Tonight, a night of success, he refused to think about that. Eden was right. A time for celebration.

Gathering his crutches, Rio pushed to his feet. "Congratulations. You've made a lot of people happy."

Including him.

Eden followed him to the door and stood in the entry as he started down the two steps. Once he reached the bottom, he felt compelled to look at her once more. A sweet picture for his dreams.

Backlit by the inner salon, she stood on the top step, Brinkley at her side. Rio stood below her, bringing them close to the same height. Everything in Rio wanted to take her in his arms, but the crutches were a problem.

Being a problem solver and a man of action, he said, "I'm feeling celebratory. Mind if kiss you?"

He saw the surprise on her face. Her mouth dropped, only enough to make him want to kiss her even more. And then her expression softened.

"I'd like that very much."

Letting one crutch fall to the dry grass with a thud, he used the other as leverage to lean in close. With his free arm, he circled her small shoulders and drew her to him.

Her unique scent of shampoo, cologne and peppermint circled through his senses, an intoxicating mixture.

"There has to be a better way," he murmured and was rewarded with her tiny giggle. The sound was all he needed.

He pressed his mouth to hers, felt her sigh, and, even as he relished the touch and warmth and peppermint taste of her, Rio suspected he was in trouble. Serious trouble.

Chapter Ten

Eden wasn't a teenager. She'd been kissed before. But never like this. Never by a man who held himself with such restraint, hard shoulder muscles tense, as if he feared hurting her.

As if she were precious and fragile.

Tenderness swamped her. He was so much bigger and stronger, but Eden felt the overwhelming need to take care of him.

Didn't everyone need someone to look after his best interests, even an army ranger who was obviously more than he appeared?

Or was her attraction sending her imagination into high gear?

Probably.

Ending a kiss that had barely begun, she murmured, "I won't break."

A wry quirk pushed up the corners of his mouth. He wobbled slightly and said, "I might."

A laugh bubbled inside Eden and made its way to the surface. "You're going to fall."

Those lips, those amazingly tender lips, curved. "Will you save me?"

"Absolutely."

His expression grew serious, his tone hinting at a deeper meaning. "I believe you would."

He stared into her face as if to memorize every part and every nuance. Then once more, his gaze fell to her mouth.

Anticipation tingled Eden's skin. Her heartbeat picked up speed. Her breath shortened.

December was supposed to be cold but she grew as warm as springtime.

Rio's strong fingers tilted her chin. His minty breath whispered against her mouth. Goose bumps rose on her skin.

And then he kissed her again. Although he still held her with restrained strength, the kiss deepened, asking questions that set her heart afire.

Eden returned the kiss as sensations sailed through her on a river of wishes she knew would not—could not—come true. Yet, her heart beat stronger, louder, and rose into her throat.

She wanted the sweet moment to go on and on, but of course, it could not. A celebratory kiss was not a declaration of love. Love with Rio—a mysterious man on the move, a man of no faith—was out of the question.

So, what in the world was she doing? Had her good sense left the building?

Resolved but reluctant, Eden ended the kiss but didn't move away. A dozen conflicting thoughts raced through her head…and her heart.

She liked Rio more than she'd liked any man in a long time.

With a sigh, Rio rested his chin on her head. "I should go."

Was he as reluctant as she to say goodnight? "We're both exhausted."

"Yeah." But he didn't release her. And she didn't release him.

Somewhere on the block, a car door slammed. An engine started. Oncoming lights panned the street beside her salon.

Gripping his one crutch, Rio placed a soft kiss on her hair and stepped away.

To cover an unexpected ache from the loss of his nearness, Eden retrieved the other crutch.

Sliding it under his arm, Rio pivoted away. He tilted his head toward Grandpa's back door and the light glowing yellow from the porch. "Lock up. I'll wait until you're in the house to leave."

"No need. I'm safe here." *Except from you, and that danger is to my heart.*

He faced her again, sighed. Beneath the neatly trimmed beard, his jaw flexed.

"Go. Please."

A protector. A warrior. Who'd kissed her as if his life depended on it.

As weary as she was, Rio's broken leg must make him more so, and he wouldn't budge until she was safe.

So Eden did as he asked, locking up the salon while he stood sentry in the Christmas-lit shadows.

She'd taken care of herself and others for so long, she'd long since stopped being afraid of the dark. God was with her.

But tonight, having Rio nearby felt incredibly comforting.

If she wasn't careful, she'd fall in love with him. Maybe she was already headed in that direction. A foolish journey for sure.

You cannot fall in love with this man, her conscience said, reiterating the valid reasons, the most important one being her faith and his lack thereof.

She knew that, had lived the decision with conviction all of her life. This week, the words had become a mantra she'd repeated often.

To this enigmatic man, she was only a temporary distraction. Still, she firmly believed God had put him in her life for a reason. A reason that couldn't be about love. Not the kissing kind, anyway.

Yet she'd let him kiss her, had kissed him in return.

If the swirling emotions inside her chest were any indication, she had a lot to pray about.

Normally an easy sleeper, Rio tossed, turned and pounded the pillow for a long time after returning to the hotel. Kissing Eden was the dumbest thing he'd done in a long time. He'd always been able to control his emotions, regardless of how much he liked someone, particularly when the liking involved an attractive woman.

But Eden wasn't his usual kind of woman. She

was good, sweet, small-town, the marrying kind. He was none of those things. Compared to Eden Carnegie, he felt old and worldly. Unworthy. A guy like him would extinguish the light in those happy eyes of hers so fast she'd never know what hit her.

If she knew how truly dark he could be, she'd never have let him touch her.

Yet she had. She'd kissed him as if he mattered to her.

He'd been about as lost as he'd ever been in his life. A simple chaste kiss, which he'd foolishly called "celebratory," had rocked his world.

It was the giggle that had wiped him out. He'd started out just fine. A quick, soft kiss in an awkward, one-legged position. Then she'd giggled, bringing a smile to his lips, a transfer of delight from her lips to his. Mixed-up fool that he was, he'd fallen into her sweetness so far and so fast he'd almost drowned.

His heart had nearly jumped through his skin.

He'd heard the tiny hitch in her breath, exulted when she'd tried her best to move closer to him. Despite their position on the steps with only one crutch to keep him from thudding on his face like a felled pine tree, or perhaps because of it, she'd held him steady and kissed him back.

Oh, man, had she ever kissed him.

Closing his eyes, he relived the moments of holding her halfway in his arms. If he had the choice to do it all over, he would. Only he'd find a less awkward position so he could hold her close and feel her heart talking to his.

He should probably thank God for the awkward position—which proved another way Eden had invaded his senses. She had him thinking about God, Jesus, religion.

He didn't want to hurt her. She was too...precious...a word he'd never used to describe anyone before.

Punching the pillow again, Rio growled, "It was only a kiss." Not his best at that, given the situation.

Why was he agonizing over it? He'd never given a romantic encounter so much as a second thought.

Maybe that was the problem. Eden was different and he'd known it the moment she'd bopped into the hospital ER in her Santa hat, shining bright as the sun, concerned about his well-being.

He'd been enchanted.

From that point on, he hadn't been able to stay away from her.

He wasn't even working an op. He could gain exactly nothing from spending more time with Eden Carnegie, from getting to know her better.

In a few weeks, he planned to be long gone.

The thought comforted him. A few weeks. He was a professional. He could handle anything for a couple of weeks.

Even his wayward heart.

Sunday morning, after a better sleep than she'd expected, Eden called Golden Leaves to see if her mother was well enough today for church services. Sometimes she was and sometimes she wasn't. To Eden's disappointment, the nurse said Mom had had a bad night, so the hoped-for outing wouldn't happen.

"I know, Lord, I know," Eden whispered as she stood in church next to Grandpa for the opening hymn. "You're working all things for my good and Mom's, too."

Her brain understood, but her daughter's heart longed for her mother to be there at her side.

The worship team transitioned to "In Christ Alone," and Eden focused on worship and her blessings instead of things she didn't have.

"Thank You, Father, that we can give Christmas to more veterans than ever this year," she whispered, eyes closed. "Thank You for this caring, giving community that came out in force yesterday. Bless them all. Thank You that Grandpa can still stand for prayer and worship music. All because of Your great mercy and love."

With a grateful spirit, she went on enumerating every blessing she could name. God was great. Her life was good.

Sometimes she just needed a little reminder.

Taffy, who seemed to always be late for church, slid in beside her and leaned close. "Did you notice the tall, dark, handsome dude in the back?"

Leave it to Taffy to scope out the good-looking men as she found her way to a seat. Eden shook her head, trying to stay focused on the worship music.

Taffy, on the other hand, was not finished. "Did you invite him?"

"Who?" She kept her voice low, although the music was loud enough to cover a full-voiced conversation.

Making a funny face and trying to be subtle, Taffy twitched her head toward the back. "Your guy. Rio."

"Rio's here?" The whisper came out louder than she'd intended. She fought hard not to turn around and look, but a thrill raced through her.

"Looking like Sunday dessert."

Eden bit her lip against a giggle and elbowed the photographer. "Hush."

Taffy grinned, unrepentant, but turned her attention to the overhead screen and the words to "House of the Lord."

Eden, on the other hand, lost focus for the remainder of the service. All she could think about, and pray about, was Rio. Was he really there? In church?

Speak to his heart, Lord. Heal his brokenness, whatever it is. Show him that You're real.

When church ended, she cast what she hoped was a furtive glance toward the row Taffy indicated. Her pulse jumped. Laser-blue eyes stared directly at her.

Quickly, she handed her Bible to Grandpa. "Rio Hendrix is here. I want to see him before he slips out."

"Go. I'll catch up."

Squeezing past Taffy—the woman with the Cheshire Cat grin—Eden hurried to where Rio stood, leaning on both crutches. Some of the church members had stopped to welcome him, although he looked uncomfortable, as if he'd never been in a church.

She knew he had. Miss Mamie had been a stickler for church attendance. If a boy lived in her house, he attended church somewhere—his choice, but he attended.

Yet, Rio had never been a believer, and he'd been away from Miss Mamie's influence a long, long time.

Zoey, John-Parker and a half dozen teenage boys reached Rio before she did. John-Parker gripped his hand and slapped him on the back.

When she reached him, Rio held both hands out as if to say, *I don't know how this happened either.*

But she knew. She prayed for him morning and night. Jesus was drawing him to the Truth.

Oh, she was so happy she could shout.

Instead, she smiled into his handsome face and said the obvious. "I'm glad you came. We had a long night last night."

"A good one, though."

John-Parker glanced from her to Rio and back. "Something going on I should know about?"

Heat rushed over Eden's neck and face. "Cleaning up and counting money, John-Parker."

Followed by a sweet, head-spinning, goodnight kiss.

"Ah, the Paw Spa thing. That's right. How did you come out?"

"Great," Rio answered. "But you're welcome to add to the coffers if the spirit moves you."

Eden appreciated Rio's ability to shift the topic away from his time with her to the "Paw Spa thing," as John-Parker termed yesterday's event.

John-Parker, winter Stetson in hand, nodded. "I'll think about it. Right now, I'm hungry. You coming to the house for—"

He looked to Zoey, who responded, "Chicken spaghetti casserole."

Rio shook his head. "Thanks, but I have other plans."

"Stop by later then. Wedding talk."

Both men grabbed their throats as if choking. Zoey teasingly whacked her fiancé on the arm. "You love it. Don't pretend."

He hooked an arm over her shoulders and pulled her to his side. "She's right. If Zoey's involved, I'm all in."

A tiny pinch of envy caught Eden by surprise. She was happy for her friends, not jealous.

The couple said their goodbyes and headed out, following the herd of teenagers who'd found friends to talk to out in the church yard.

Eden wanted to ask about Rio's Sunday dinner plans, but they were none of her business. Even though she felt as if they were.

Last night's kisses had messed with her head. "Celebratory," he'd called them. *Only* celebratory. And that was for the best.

Rio shifted on the crutches. "I need to get off this leg. Want to go out to eat with me? You and your grandpa? Clean the salon afterward? My help is pathetic but also free."

A zippy little thrill tickled Eden's stomach. She tamped it down.

Rio's was an invitation between friends. He'd included Grandpa. Plus, they had plenty of cleanup on the agenda.

Grandpa, who had greeted and shaken hands with half the church, made his way slowly to her side just as Rio'd issued his *friendly* invitation.

"Why not have dinner at our house?" Grandpa asked. "Eden's got a pot roast in the slow cooker big enough to feed Cox's Army."

Eden had never learned who Cox's Army was, but since Grandpa used the term often, it must have been big.

"With potatoes, carrots and roast beef gravy," she added. "Plus hot rolls."

"Roast beef." Rio scratched the side of his beard as if pondering. "A dish I haven't tasted in a while."

"Then you'll come?" She kept the excitement out of her voice but forgot to tell her heart.

"Can't argue with a home-cooked meal."

Though his tone was light and easy, Eden heard a note of regret in the words.

Just how alone was this man in whatever life he led outside of this one, rare visit to Rosemary Ridge?

A question she wouldn't ask, of course.

However, she *would* ask him about this morning's church attendance.

When the moment was right.

Chapter Eleven

Rio left Eden's home—and neatly cleaned salon—with a belly full of hearty beef and her granddad's cherry pie, but in a tumultuous state of mind.

Being with her, as well as her grandpa, felt comfortable and relaxed in ways he hadn't experienced in a long time. Perhaps forever. That wasn't good. Living a life of lies and spies required he remain on edge and alert at all times. One relaxed moment could get him killed and compromise the security of his country. And that of his allies, too.

Turning these concerns over in his head, Rio drove the Mustang to Mamie's House of Hope, as JP and Zoey had christened the big, three-story foster home. Brandt's Corvette was parked next to JP's giant pickup truck.

A meeting of the old gang. Except Rio didn't fit anymore.

One of the foster boys, River, who reminded Rio of himself whenever they met, opened the door. The teen's dark shaggy hair had been combed and he looked more presentable than usual. Because of church, Rio supposed. JP would insist, the way Miss Mamie had.

"Take your best to God's house," she'd say. "You're visiting the King of Kings."

River jabbed a thumb over one shoulder toward the inside of the house. "Come in."

"Good to see you again, River," Rio said.

"Yeah." Face solemn as if he feared being seen as friendly, the boy turned and skulked into the large open-concept living area. Rio understood the don't-care reaction, the need to hide all the anger and confusion whirling inside. Hadn't he once been the same?

Sometimes he still was.

Once inside, he was again reminded of how different the home was in comparison to the space where he and the other street rats had spent their teen years. Zoey and JP had taken things up a notch. Miss Mamie would be pleased.

From the other side of a large island, he heard female voices and spotted Zoey with Berkley Metcalfe, Brandt's fiancée, staring at a laptop computer. Two pretty women, nice women, though different as could be.

Good people. Like Eden.

Zoey waved toward him. "Hi, Rio. The guys are in the basement."

The basement. Rio stifled an inward groan. Stairs and crutches, not the best combo.

With a nod, he hobbled to the entrance to Zoey's

private apartments. Since the wedding was next week, JP had begun moving things in.

Taking the stairs slowly and leaning one shoulder against the wall for extra support, Rio made his way to the bottom.

From a gray couch, JP and Brandt turned their heads in his direction, away from the big-screen TV on one wall that displayed a football game. "Giants are winning."

Neither looked happy about that.

Zoey's little boy, Owen, sprawled across JP's lap, half asleep. Cute kid, he adored JP. The father need, Rio supposed, something he understood all too well.

"You should install an elevator." Rio collapsed in a cushy chair perpendicular to the couch and let the crutches fall against it. "What's the score?"

"It's 31-14, fourth quarter, three minutes. Not looking good for the Cards."

The other two men had lived in Arizona for years. He wasn't surprised they were Cardinals fans. "Sorry."

Except he wasn't really. He'd been out of country and someone else for so long, he paid little attention to American sports.

When the game ended with a Cardinal defeat as expected, JP pointed the remote and clicked off the TV. His soon-to-be son stirred. "Dad, can I have a snack?"

"Didn't you eat dinner?"

The preschooler, face twisted in fake agony, rubbed his stomach. "I'm still hungry."

"Come on then. You can have some fruit."

"Gummy fruits?" the boy asked hopefully.

JP laughed. "We'll talk about it." To the other men, he said, "Zoey keeps snacks and drinks down here in the mini-kitchen. Want something?"

He circled around the small island dividing the living space from the kitchenette and opened the fridge. "Cokes, tea, water?"

"Water's good," Rio said.

"Tea for me. I'll get it." Brandt, still dressed for church, retrieved a glass of sweet tea and Rio's water before returning to the couch.

JP and the little boy disappeared into the back and returned with a plastic bucket of toy cars. Owen dumped them on the rug and sat down to play while eating his banana. JP reclaimed his spot on the couch.

"How'd you like church this morning?" JP pointed a soda at him.

"It was all right." The music hadn't been bad, but the preacher's sermon had seemed to hit him between the eyes. All that "Jesus died for your sins" business had stirred something in his gut that two Tums hadn't touched.

Plus, he'd struggled to keep his attention off Eden. He still didn't know why he'd gone. Boredom, he supposed.

"Zoey and I host a Bible study here on Tuesday evenings. Want to join us?"

Rio stared at his bottle of water. "Not my thing."

"Wasn't mine either."

"Or mine," Brandt added.

No, it hadn't been. They'd been three rabble-rousers who'd done their best to avoid church. But JP and Brandt had different lives now. He didn't.

"Too much to live up to." He tried for a short self-deprecating laugh, though his words were as true as anything in his life. And that wasn't much, come to think of it. "I'm not that good."

Feeling JP's stare against his skin, Rio added, "You don't know me anymore, JP."

"Jesus does. He knows everything about you, everything you've done, where you've been, how you feel. He *knows* you." JP set his Coke on an end table and leaned forward, forearms resting on his thighs, quietly earnest. "Here's the deal, Rio. None of us can ever be good enough to deserve God's grace and forgiveness. That's why Jesus came. *His* goodness is all we need."

Rio tried for a snicker. "What are you now, a preacher?"

"Zoey and I ask him that all the time," Brandt said. "Brace yourself, Rio. He's unstoppable."

"Because I care." JP waved his soda can. "We grew up together, remember? Foster kids. I know some of the junk you carry around. Same way Brandt and I did. Jesus was the only answer that worked for either of us. Still is."

"You were the nice ones." Resisting the strange pull inside his chest, Rio ran his fingers down the damp plastic bottle and kept his tone light, slightly bored. The way he did in an op. *Never let 'em see you sweat.* "I was the guy pounding heads."

"You still doing that?"

How did he answer that honestly?

The same way he did in an op. Evasion.

"Look, I'm glad religion works for you but it wouldn't for me. My job requires things of me—" Rio stopped. He was talking too much. This morning's church service haunted him. The words the pastor had said—and now JP was saying some of the same—made him wish he was more like his friends, like Eden, and less like himself.

Using evasive intelligence techniques against his buddies grated on his conscience. He wanted to spill his guts and trust someone just once in his life besides himself.

Yet he couldn't.

JP clapped a hand on his knee. "War made all of us question our humanity. No doubt being in the rangers, you saw and did things you'd like to forget. Add that on top of our bizarre childhood experiences and we all have baggage."

"Can't argue." Baggage. Lots of it. Nonstop baggage. Some, like the situation with his dad, he'd come by innocently. Others, he'd signed up for.

Rio took a swig of cold water, wondering if he should try again to contact his dad...or his bosses. Wondering, too, if his friends would consider him a candidate for Christianity if they knew the dark side of his career choices.

"Don't you think it's time you let someone else help you carry yours?" JP asked.

Someone? Like Jesus? Like a God he couldn't see and had never believed in?

Shifting uneasily, he returned to habit and evaded the question. "I thought you wanted to discuss the big wedding."

Brandt pointed at him and laughed. "Good segue."

"All right, all right, let's talk wedding." JP held up both hands in surrender. "But I have a couple of books I'd like you to read. Will you do that?"

"Sure." Knowledge was power. He liked to read and could whip through any book in short order. Right now, he'd agree to anything to change the subject.

"Great." JP slapped both knees. "I'm praying for you, pal. Remember that."

How could he forget? Eden had said the same thing before he'd left her house.

Snow flurries swirled from a white-gray sky on the wedding day of John-Parker Wisdom and Zoey Chavez. Though the ground remained too warm for any of the fluffy stuff to stick, snow was pretty and Eden loved it. Snow made her happy. Weddings made her happy. The two together were happiness on steroids.

And if she were honest with herself, Rio's invitation to ride with him to the wedding filled her with extra special delight. She hadn't even bothered to analyze his reasons. After all, he'd also invited her grandfather, but the colder, moister air had exacerbated Grandpa's breathing issues and he'd opted out of the wedding.

Even as she chided herself for caring too much, she spent extra time dressing for the evening wedding. She'd bought the red wrap dress on sale last year after the holidays, but the strappy heels and gold-tone jewelry were new. She'd even had her fingernails painted at the nail spa, a mostly hopeless task considering her occupation, but the red color matched her dress and the delicate snowflake designs made her smile.

"What do you think, Brinkley?"

The little dog watched her every move with tilted head, as if wondering if she'd dress him up and take him along.

"Not this time, sweetie. You stay and keep Grandpa company."

She took another turn in the full-length mirror, adjusted the belt sash and checked the back of her hair. Tucked behind one ear to show off a dangly earring, the easy waves fell to her shoulders.

"Good enough." Definitely better than her usual dog groomer smock and ponytail.

With a final spritz of perfume, she slid into her black heels and went to answer the knock on the door.

Dog tags jingling like Christmas bells, Brinkley shot out of the room before her.

Rio was here. If her heart beat a little faster, she let it. Today was a special day and she felt pretty.

"You've got company," Grandpa hollered from the living room. Apparently, he, along with Brinkley, had beat her to the door.

"Grandpa, you shouldn't exert yourself. I could have gotten—"

The words died in her throat at the sight of Rio Hendrix standing in her living room in a black tux and crisp white shirt accented by a red tie. His usually shaggy hair was trimmed and styled. His barely-there beard neatly framed his perfect bone structure and drew attention to those startling blue eyes.

With the smirk on his lips and the air of danger he carried like a shield, the man could play James Bond in a movie.

The women in his world must fall all over him.

"You look gorgeous," he said while she was still finding her voice.

To hide the blush that heated her face, Eden faked a curtsy. "Thank you, sir. You look very handsome yourself."

Understatement of the millennium.

With Brinkley dancing around his one gleaming black shoe and the black boot cast, Rio touched the red tie. "We match, even without your Santa hat."

Eden laughed. "We do. Look at you being all Christmassy."

The smirk deepened. "Don't want to shame my friends. Theirs *is* a Christmas wedding."

He crouched to ruffle Brinkley's ears. The dog flopped onto his back in ecstasy, begging for a belly scratch. And received one.

Interesting that Rio would care about dressing for the occasion when he claimed not to like Christmas. Was he softening? Or play-acting for the sake of his friends?

The last thought caught her up short as she turned it over in her mind, pondering. On the outside, he was social, friendly, even charming, but who was the real Rio Hendrix on the inside?

"I'll grab my coat and purse," she said, worrying with the realization of how little she knew about the man on whom she'd developed a crush.

When she returned, Rio took the coat, leaned his crutches against the wall, and held the wrap while she slipped it on. Eden thought of 007 again. Very continental. Suavely courteous. And dangerously mysterious.

Oh, my heart. Stop that right now.

Blue eyes bored into hers. "Ready?"

"Yes." She took her black sparkly clutch bag from the chair where she'd dropped it to slip into her coat.

Oxygen tank in tow, Grandpa stood at the door and spoke to Rio. "Weather's tricky. Watch your speed. You're carrying precious cargo."

Rio dipped his chin, face serious. "You have my word, sir."

"Good enough. And bring me some cake," Grandpa said with a wheezing laugh.

As if to prove he'd take care of her—an unnecessary but altogether lovely action—Rio somehow managed to manipulate the crutches and pull her hand into the crook of his elbow. "Hold on."

"I could say the same for you."

His teeth flashed. "Teamwork."

They made it safely to the car and drove the short distance to the church.

As they entered the sanctuary, Charlie, one of John-Parker's foster teens, greeted them.

"I'm an usher," he said proudly. "Me and River."

"Looking good, Charlie."

"Zoey made me wear this suit. It's okay but the tie is choking me to death." He tugged at the noose, twisting his head in the universal sign for a too tight tie.

"Here, my man. Let me help." As serious as if he were performing brain surgery, Rio adjusted the boy's tie and finished up with a double chest pat. "How's that? Better?"

Charlie's face brightened. "I can breathe!" He stood a bit taller. "May I escort you to your preferred side? Zoey made me memorize that line. Did I do okay?"

"Excellent," Rio said. "Could not have done better myself."

Grinning proudly, the sweet-natured teen led them to a greenery-draped row of chairs.

Eden waved or smiled her way down the left aisle of the church. Neither bride nor groom had a biological family to share in their joy so Eden was particularly pleased to see a good number of friends in attendance.

She paused to hug an elderly couple, friends of her grandfather's and the late Miss Mamie's, and then turned in the row of chairs to trade handclasps with a family seated behind them.

"Do you know everyone in town?" Rio slid his crutches lengthwise down the row.

"Mostly," she said and settled onto a cushioned chair. "I love people."

"And dogs." Rio teased. "Lots of dogs. Dangerous dogs who break a man's legs."

"You'll never let me forget that, will you?"

He pulled a long face and pressed a hand to his heart. "I'm traumatized for life."

"Are you really?"

"No. If not for the accident, I wouldn't be here with you." From the gleam in his eye, being with her was a good thing.

"See how that works?" She beamed at him. "Without the accident, we'd still be strangers. And the veterans' committee wouldn't have the funds for our big celebration."

One black eyebrow shot up. "So you're saying God broke my leg?"

"No!" Then realizing she was too loud, Eden squinched her shoulders together and whispered, "Sorry. But, no, God didn't cause the accident. He simply redeemed it, like He does us."

Before they could continue, the pianist began

to play and the buzz of congregational conversation quieted.

Eden leaned close to Rio's ear and whispered, "I'm truly sorry for the broken leg, but not for our friendship." Nor for the softening she'd noticed in Rio over their short acquaintance.

Rio turned his head enough that, in the crowded space, they were eyeball to eyeball. Voice soft, he murmured, "Just giving you a hard time. Did I mention that you look exceptionally beautiful?"

He switched topics so quickly sometimes she got whiplash. And he was so close in the narrow confines of the seats that she could count his eyelashes and see the navy blue rims around his eyes.

He had such stunning eyes. Last night, they'd invaded her dreams.

She swallowed, fought down the sudden thunder of pulse against her collarbone. They were in church. This was no time to think about the crush she'd developed on Rio Hendrix.

Pretending she was not at all affected by his nearness, she whispered, "The church is gorgeous, isn't it?"

To prove she could stop thinking about Rio and switch topics the way he did, she turned her attention to the Christmas wedding décor.

Tall, multilight candelabras festooned with red-and-white tulle bows lined the left and right sides of the front, their safety candles already aglow. In between, an archway of white flowers and tiny fairy lights was bracketed with bunches of red poinsettias surrounded by more fairy lights. Directly beneath the archway, the white-draped prayer table and unity candle awaited the bride and groom. Finally, tall Christmas trees lit only with white lights stood sentry at the sides of the platform.

"A Christmas wonderland, if you're into that kind of thing." The cynicism was back in his voice.

"I love it. Everything is so...so... Christmassy!" She knew she stated the obvious but used any reason to get him to notice the beauty in her favorite holiday. "I've never attended a Christmas wedding. Have you?"

"Never." He turned away then and grew quiet, as if her comments bothered him. She supposed they had. Christmas and church weren't his favorite topics.

But he was there. In a church. At a Christmas wedding. And he'd attended church last Sunday.

Positives, every single one.

The music changed and a dreamlike melody began to fill the sanctuary. The ceremony must be about to begin. Eden turned her full attention away from Rio to the front of the church.

Pastor Everly, John-Parker and Brandt appeared from behind the stage and stepped into place beneath the archway. Hands folded in front of them, both big, brave bodyguards looked slightly nervous but stunningly handsome in their tuxedoes that looked much like the one Rio wore. Right down to the red tie and pocket square. She wondered if Rio's attire had been John-Parker's request or his own idea. The man knew how to dress for the occasion, that was for certain.

The pianist smoothly moved to Pachelbel's *Canon in D Major*, a signal for the entrance of the maid of honor. Although Taffy was the official photographer, she was also Zoey's closest friend and only attendant. She came down the aisle in a one-shouldered, red-velvet gown, carrying a nosegay of evergreens and holly.

Zoey's children, Owen and Olivia, as flower fairy and ring bearer, followed. One-year-old Olivia took one look at the gathering, dropped the basket of flower petals and raced the rest of the way to John-Parker. Her almost-dad lifted her in his arms, kissed her on the cheek and told her she was beautiful. The little girl clung to his neck and buried her face in his shoulder. He patted her back and smiled toward Owen.

Eden's heart melted.

John-Parker loved those kids.

*Some*day, if God granted, she wanted a darling pair like those two and a husband who loved them and her.

Someday.

A resolute Owen picked up his sister's basket and marched onward, dutifully scattering the rose petals Olivia had left behind until he reached John-Parker's side.

Taffy, ever practical, extracted Olivia from the groom. But when she reached for Owen's hand, the little boy said, "No, Taffy. I have Mommy's ring. I have to be still. Dad said so."

The wedding party laughed. Owen looked bewildered but remained staunchly at John-Parker's side.

Eden joined the collective chuckles but quieted when the pianist played the introductory notes of the "Bridal Chorus."

The wedding guests stood and turned toward Zoey. Eden's Christmas-loving brain captured every beautiful detail.

Glowing with joy, eyes glued to her groom, the bride came down the aisle alone in cream-colored lace sashed in Christmas red to match the men's ties. She carried a bouquet of red and cream roses interspersed with pinecones, holly and snowy evergreens.

Eden couldn't help it. She sighed an admiring, "Oh."

Beside her, Rio shifted, turning his attention first on her, with a slight tilt of his mouth, and then to the men in front.

Eden followed his gaze to John-Parker. The tough-guy bodyguard blinked glassy eyes, his expression enraptured.

Longing expanded in Eden's heart.

She was delighted for her friends. But would a bridegroom ever look at her with that much love and joy?

Without thinking through the action, she gazed up at Rio, saw the caring and, perhaps, a yearning, in his unguarded expression.

Those two men in front had once been his only family, and regardless of the time in between, they still mattered to him a great deal. Did he wish he could be more like them? That he could settle down somewhere and find a forever family of his own, the way John-Parker and Brandt were doing?

Or was he simply happy for his friends but eager to be on his way to somewhere else?

He must have felt her stare because, as the bride reached her groom, Rio glanced down at Eden. Their gazes locked for a few heart-pounding seconds in which she inwardly acknowledged a secret envy of her friend's beautiful love. She wanted that, too. More than she ever had before.

She, a woman with strict falling-in-love rules, was in serious danger of getting her heart broken by Rio Hendrix.

Chapter Twelve

Rio had attended plenty of weddings, most of them culturally different from JP and Zoey's traditional Christian nuptials. None of them had gotten to him the way this one had. Sure, he was happy for his friends, if this is what they wanted, but he suspected the real reason for his mushy insides was the small woman at his side.

When Eden had walked into her living room, beautiful in red, with her dark hair tumbling over her shoulders, she'd dazzled him. Truth was, she dazzled him every bit as much in her doggy smocks and Santa hats. Eden Carnegie, with her dimples, positive outlook and altruistic heart, was a very special woman.

Some guy somewhere was missing out. Not him. He couldn't get involved any deeper than he already was.

And he'd gotten in pretty deep, considering that he couldn't seem to stay away from Miss Merry Christmas.

He'd also wrestled with his growing feelings enough to know that he was not her future. She deserved more. Better. She deserved everything he wasn't.

But he could enjoy her company while he was in town.

Satisfied that he'd made the right decision, he tore his gaze away from Eden's wholesome prettiness and tuned in to the wedding ceremony. The stirring of regret didn't surprise him. He was human. If life had been different, if he'd grown up in a normal, healthy environment, he'd want the same things other men wanted. A wife. Family. Cute kids like the pair at the altar with Zoey and JP.

A little girl in fluffy dresses with brown eyes and ocean-deep dimples. Or doggy smocks and ponytails.

He clapped a lid on the troublesome thoughts and listened in as his friends exchanged promises to love and to honor.

This was good. Very good. JP finally had the one thing lacking in his life—in all the street rats' lives. A family of his own.

A lump formed in Rio's throat. Whether regret for himself or happiness for his friend, he didn't know. Maybe both.

He'd made his choices years ago and had never looked back. No need to start now.

When Eden sniffled, he reached for her hand, intending to release her fingers after a quick squeeze. But when she folded her fingers over his, he changed his mind and held on.

Enjoy her company while he could. Wasn't that his decision?

Just like every other woman he'd known, she'd soon be part of his past.

Because she'd hate him if she knew who he really was.

Seated at a white-clothed table in the church's family center, Eden swayed to the music of "A Thousand Years" as John-Parker waltzed his new bride around the reception floor. Laughing into each other's eyes, they occasionally paused to rub noses or exchange a kiss to the hoots of the attending friends.

This was their first dance as man and wife, and their obvious love for one another almost made Eden teary again.

Not that she regretted the sentimental moment during the ceremony that had caused Rio to reach for her hand and hold it securely against his thigh. She didn't. In fact, she'd loved the gentle strength of his much longer fingers wrapped around hers.

When her stomach fluttered and her head filled with warm and tender thoughts, she'd let it. *Weddings*, she told herself, *cause all kinds of romantic, sentimental emotions*. And she was having plenty of them today.

For the last week, too.

A tiny sigh escaped her lips. Her eyes strayed to the handsome but admittedly unsuitable man seated next to her. He was in her prayers constantly as she tried to understand what God expected from her in this situation. He'd obviously put Rio in her life, to share her faith with him, to show him kindness and the spiritual beauty of Christmas, but He surely hadn't intended for her to fall in love with the man.

The bridal couple's first dance ended and the DJ urged everyone to join them on the floor.

Disappointment pinched Eden. She hadn't danced since the last wedding she'd attended two years ago, but the only man she wanted to dance with tonight was the man on crutches.

Since dancing couldn't happen, Eden stood and asked, "Would you like something from the buffet?"

"No." One eyebrow lifted, he aimed his look toward the dance floor. "What I'd like is to dance with you."

She stared down at his booted leg. "I don't think that's possible."

"What? You've never seen anyone trip the light fantastic on crutches?"

Eden chuckled. "No."

"Today is the day, m'lady." Taking the crutches, he pushed to a stand. When he saw her hesitation, he grew serious. "If this is going to embarrass you, I'll rescind my invitation."

His thoughtful respect for her feelings clinched the deal.

"Me?" She pointed two decorated fingernails toward herself. "Embarrassed? A woman who wears reindeer antlers to the grocery store?"

His lips tilted. "Do you really?"

"What do you think? Of course, I do. It's Christmas, and even without reindeer antlers, I would love to dance with you. The question is, Would *you* dance with *me* if I wore them?"

Humor lit his gaze but he contemplated, as if the question were of national significance. "Not today. They wouldn't match your dress."

Suddenly buzzed with renewed energy, Eden laughed. "Come on. Show me what you've got."

A plethora of other couples moseyed onto the floor, so Rio nudged his chin toward an emptier corner. "Looks like my favorite spot is over there. Safety."

She tucked her hand around the elbow he offered and matched her steps to his crutches just as the DJ spun the classic fast tune, "Footloose."

Rio paused, cocked his head. "I think they're playing our song!"

"Because you wish your foot was loose?"

He wagged his boot cast. "You got it."

When they arrived in the less crowded corner, Eden dropped her hold on his elbow and asked, "How should we go about this? I don't want to be the only one dancing while you stand and watch."

"I wouldn't mind that, but I have a plan."

"Gotta love a man with a plan." Eden hoped Rio took the casual phrase as the teasing it was, but a blush heated her cheeks anyway.

Leaning his underarms on the crutches, her

handsome escort offered a hand. "Consider me the anchor and I'll twirl you around, jitterbug style."

Though dubious, Eden placed her hand in his. "I'm willing to try if you are." No matter how silly they might look.

Holding to his fingertips, Eden bee-bopped under his arm and in circles around him while he swayed to the music and tapped his one shiny black shoe.

After a few spins, they found their rhythm and danced in humorous, energetic style to another fast song. Eden laughed and Rio smirked. Seeing the dark, broody man enjoy himself thrilled her. He even laughed a few times. And she laughed a lot.

"This is way more fun than I imagined." Gripping his fingertips, she jitterbugged toward him, breath coming in happy puffs.

"I'm a regular one-man entertainment system," Rio teased and twirled her behind his back for good measure.

She couldn't argue with that. She found him vastly entertaining, and if their trips to the veterans' home were any indication, so did the residents he befriended. Chess, checkers, dominoes...whatever they wanted to do, he was all in.

Beneath that cynical, broken facade was a nice man. And *that* was the problem her heart was having.

When the next song ended, Eden didn't want to leave the floor, but she also didn't want Rio to hurt himself.

As she turned to walk back to her chair against

one wall, Rio caught her fingertips and tugged her back. "Want to try another?"

Yes, she did. Time spent with Rio invigorated her, recharged her happy batteries.

"Are you sure you're up to the task?"

"Always."

She believed him. Whatever he did in his other life, she had no doubt that he did the job with everything in him.

Another familiar fast track blared from the DJ stand. The old '70s Bee Gees' classic "Staying Alive."

Apparently seeing the irony, Rio shook his head toward the ceiling. "I'm trying to. Tell it to runaway dogs and a certain elf."

Eden put a hand to her quivering lips. She loved his humor. For such a serious man, he knew how to have fun.

She struck a pose, one arm stretched out in a point. "Show me your John Travolta finger-pointing moves."

"Oh, yeah. I have some. Let's go."

Over the next three minutes, their dancing was delightfully terrible. Neither of them knew the actual dance steps, which made the effort even more fun. The results consisted mostly of finger points, arm rolls and drawing two fingers across their eyes. And laughing a lot.

At one point, as she bopped around him, Rio tried a one-legged turn to follow her circular motion. Halfway around, he lost his balance and began to wobble. Eden's hands shot out, intending to stabilize him, but she wound up with her arms around him instead.

In the melee, Rio's crutches tumbled to the floor. He clasped one hand to her shoulder for balance and circled her waist with the other.

Stunned, she backed slightly away without turning loose. She didn't want him to fall. But he was close. Real close.

His subtle woodsy-spiced cologne invaded her senses, expensive and tantalizing. Mysterious, too, like him, and utterly masculine.

"I think I like this next dance better," he murmured while the smooth voice of Michael Bublé crooned, "When I Fall in Love."

Eden's pulse, still pounding from the lively dances, picked up the pace even more.

She swallowed. Tried not to listen to the beautiful, romantic words that gave her all kinds of unsettling thoughts. "Hold on while I get your crutches."

He drew her back. "Leave them."

"But you're not supposed to—"

"No arguments." His smile, and that one hiked eyebrow, were a challenge. "You broke my leg and now you have to slow dance with me as punishment."

Slow dancing with Rio would only be a punishment because this was all the closeness they could ever have together. "You'll hurt yourself."

"Should be healed by now."

"Are you sure?" He hadn't been in town long enough for a bone to heal. "I don't think so."

"Come on. Allow me one dance with a beautiful elf where I can stand on my own two feet."

"Promise you'll rest afterward?"

"No. But humor me."

Eden gave into the request. She hoped he was telling the truth and that his leg was, indeed, well enough for one easy waltz.

And that her heart could bear the strain of falling for the wrong kind of man.

Tomorrow, Rio thought, he would remind himself of why anything but silly fast dances with Eden Carnegie was a bad idea. A slow waltz with her was dangerous; a concern that had nothing to do with the healing bone and everything to do with facing the facts.

The love word wasn't in his vocabulary, but he had feelings for Eden Carnegie. Serious feelings.

Although, at first, she stood at a chaste distance, only connecting with him at the shoulder and hand in a traditional waltz position, Rio soaked in her touch, her sweet face and genuine joy. The smiles she flashed. The dimples that melted him. Her inner light that drew him like a beacon in the darkness. Eden was water to a dying man's soul.

Or, in his case, to a man without a soul.

The laughter of the fast dances disappeared as other couples swirled by to the romantic music. He hadn't given the words to this particular song any attention at first, but now, with Eden in his arms looking at him with affection and pleasure, he did.

The cynic in him didn't believe everlasting love was possible. The man in him longed for it to be.

With his hand at her waist, he took one step closer. His lower leg protested, but learning ballroom dance had been part of his training. A spy never knew where he'd end up. Among the wealthy and corrupt was not unusual since they were often funding the bad actors Rio stole intelligence from. A smooth dance step added protection and interest to his cover story, whatever that might be.

Not that he'd needed ballroom dance recently. Except for tonight when he wanted an excuse to hold Eden in his arms more than anything he could think of. For once, he was himself. Rio Hendrix. Not a nonexistent pseudonym among people who'd prefer the real Rio Hendrix was dead.

He moved in, felt the shift of Eden's hand from his shoulder to curve her arm around his upper back and touch his neck. Her gaze lifted to his and, trained to read people, he saw the tenderness she couldn't hide. Tenderness for him.

His heart lurched painfully. Eden was not a woman to hide her feelings. She cared for him. Maybe more than cared.

When she leaned her cheek against his shoulder, he thought he might go into tachycardia.

He cared for her, too. Too much to do anything more than enjoy her companionship on a temporary basis. He was who he was. He'd made his choices.

Love was not in the equation.

To stop the free flow of wishful romantic thoughts, Rio raised their joined hands and turned Eden gently around. Her dimples flashed. As she circled, her flowery scent wrapped around his head, mocking his efforts to stop thinking of Eden as more than a short-term friend.

He was a man of powerful self-discipline. A man trained to stand strong no matter the torture.

But they hadn't taught him what to do about a sunshine-and-goodness woman like Eden. A woman who ignited a blazing fire of impossible dreams.

The ultimate torture was love he could neither give nor accept.

Eden slipped off her heels in Rio's car, leaned back against the passenger seat and exhaled a happy aah.

"I had the best time." Because of him. But she didn't say that. "Thank you. *And* for braving the dance floor for my sake."

"Couldn't let anyone else snatch the prettiest girl in the room. I hope I didn't embarrass you."

"You didn't. I had fun. *So* much fun."

When he'd insisted on the slow dance, she'd known he'd felt more for her than he'd been ready to say. That fact worried her, but she trusted God's plan in bringing them together. Whatever it was. She was still sorting out her part, wondering if God had sent Rio for his sake or to test her faith.

Eden left the worry for later when she'd be alone to talk to God. Tonight had been too wonderful for fretting,

"Aren't John-Parker and Zoey perfect for each other? And the way they danced together. So smooth. So romantic." She clutched a hand to her chest. "They must have taken lessons from Berkley Metcalfe."

Rio gave her a quick glance. "I'd forgotten Berkley danced professionally."

"Dance teacher now. She has a studio here in Rosemary Ridge." Turning in the seat, Eden angled her knees toward him. "Are you sure your leg is okay?"

Three fingers raised and lowered on the steering wheel as if to shoo away her concern. "Fine."

She gave him a mock glower. "There's a difference between fine and good."

"Let's leave it at fine." He winked in her direction.

So, his leg *did* hurt. "I'm praying you didn't do any damage."

"I suppose prayer won't hurt anything."

The surprising statement encouraged her. In spite of his cynicism toward religion, Rio was open-minded. Eden had a neighbor like that. Though espousing atheism, the neighbor had once asked Eden to pray for him before he went into heart surgery.

"Prayer makes all the difference in the world."

Please, Lord, let him heal without problems and prove to him that You listen and care.

She didn't know why God answered some prayers with a yes and others with a no, but she still believed taking her needs to God was a powerful weapon.

Rio grew quiet, his attention on the street, but there was a subtle change in the atmosphere at the mention of prayer. A pensive tension. Almost a longing.

Though she wondered what was going on inside that brilliant head of his, Eden moved the conversation to safer ground. She was not about to get in the way of whatever God was doing in Rio's heart.

"The reception buffet was amazing, wasn't it? I don't think I'll ever be hungry again."

"Not even for ice cream?"

"Ice cream could possibly be the exception."

"Want to stop at Braum's?"

Spend more time in Rio's company? Yes, she wanted that. But a little voice inside stopped her from agreeing. "I wish I could say yes, but I really should get home. Work tomorrow."

"Right. Sure." He didn't sound disappointed. "Do you have a lot of appointments?"

"Fifteen."

"That many?"

"The number sounds daunting, but several aren't full grooms. Just holiday spruce-ups. I'll squeeze them in."

"You work hard."

Eden smiled. "It's not work when you love your job."

"True." He nodded, stared on the shadowy street ahead. "But it is admirable. You juggle a lot."

"Do you like your job?"

"It has its good points."

He didn't sound too convincing.

"Now that the wedding is over, will you go back to work right away?" Wherever and whatever his job was.

"Time will tell."

No answer at all, but she wasn't surprised. He kept his job and life outside of Rosemary Ridge close to the vest. Very close.

Conversation lulled as they turned into her neighborhood where every house was decked out for Christmas.

"Oh, Rio, look. Lonnie and Tammy's house." Eden pointed to the white ranch-style brick.

The residence was a Christmas overload. Yard ornaments and lights everywhere. Giant, lighted candy canes guarded each side of the entryway. Animated gingerbread men danced in a circle on the lawn.

Rio groaned but slowed the car to a crawl so she could admire her friends' elaborate yard décor.

"I wonder if the gingerbread boys play music," she mused.

As if by her command, the passenger's-side window slid silently down.

Eden swiveled to face her companion. Though Christmas troubled him for some reason, Rio put his opinion aside for her sake.

"Can you hear the music?" she asked, hoping he'd love it, too.

"Ho-ho-ho." He didn't smile. "'Up on the Housetop.'"

"I know! Isn't that incredible? And look up there." She pointed to the housetop where a Santa sleigh and reindeer straddled the gabled roof. Santa himself appeared ready to climb down the chimney. "How cute is that?"

"Adorable." His tone was wry, but when she glanced his way again, his eyes were on her, not the rooftop.

Was he calling *her* adorable?

Pesky flutters stirred in her stomach.

Rio liked her. Eden could see the admiration in his eyes and in the way he treated her. But he was holding part of himself back, just as she was. She knew her reasons. But what were his?

"Ready to move on?" he asked.

"Yes." She could look at Christmas decorations all night, but knew most people didn't feel that way. Especially Rio. "It was thoughtful of you to stop."

One side of his mouth kicked up. "Kind of fun watching you sparkle about a fake holiday."

Eden ignored the part about Christmas being fake. "Sparkle? Do I sparkle?"

"Yes, you do. It's charming."

Pleasure shifted over her. "Oh, good. Charming is better than obnoxious. Which someone once accused me of. But that was Jared Hines in sixth grade."

"He probably had a crush on you."

"That's what Mom said, so I forgave him. I also ignored him for the rest of the year."

"Poor sap." With an amused huff, Rio turned his attention back to the street.

The rest of the way to her house, they talked of their school years. Teachers and students they both had known, including the infamous science teacher who'd spilled coffee down the tiled hallways every morning in his rush to class.

Then Rio told some funny anecdotes about his teenage hijinks with John-Parker and Brandt.

Laughing, Eden said, "Your poor teachers."

"Miss Mamie, too. We caused our share of mischief."

Rio, she knew, had attended only high school in Rosemary Ridge. When she asked where he'd gone to school prior, he launched into another "street rats" story.

His childhood seemed to be off topic. In a way, she understood. He'd been a foster kid and memories of his early days couldn't be all that great.

Still, she wished he'd share more of himself with her. Whatever had happened to put him in the social system had influenced the man he'd become. And Eden liked that man.

They reached her home and pulled into her driveway.

"Grandpa forgot to turn on the Christmas lights."

"No timer? A fanatic like you?" He put the car in Park and reached for his crutches.

"You don't have to get out."

"Yes, I do. Stay put."

"Stubborn."

He flashed an amused glance. "You don't know the half of it."

Feeling special and protected, Eden slid into her heels, picked up her clutch bag and waited until her car door swung open.

Braced on the crutches, Rio offered a hand. The low-slung sports car was a bit difficult to get out of, especially in heels.

She exited the car and they walked the short distance past her favorite decoration, the solar-lit nativity scene, to the wreath-bedecked door.

Eden paused, key in hand, and turned to face her companion. Would he kiss her, this time as a date and not a celebration? She wanted him to, though she knew she was playing with fire and headed for a hard fall.

But this man. This man... For all his suave charm and confidence, he seemed to need someone to care about him, to see through the wall he erected around himself and really know him.

Either that or she was already too far gone in love with him to think straight. She desperately wanted to see him healed, inside and out.

But only God could do that. Not her.

As if he was as reluctant as Eden was to say good-night, Rio leaned the crutches against the house and braced a hand above her head on the door facing. "Thanks for the trip down memory lane. It was nice to remember the good things for a change."

For a change. So, he carried a lot of bad memories, too.

What, she wondered, had happened to disrupt his birth family? Did they know each other well enough for her to ask?

Though her own birth family had been fractured when Dad was killed, she'd always had Mom and Grandpa. Rio had left everything behind to live with strangers in a strange town.

Her heart hurt for him. "We made some new memories tonight, though, didn't we? Good ones."

"Yeah. We did." Amused gaze tender, he studied her face as he took a lock of her hair between finger and thumb. "After I'm gone, I'll remember this night for a long time."

Eden swallowed. She knew he'd eventually leave, but right now she didn't want to think about that. "Me, too. And we'll have pictures. Taffy snapped a ton of everything, even of you and me."

"I noticed." Taking the house key from her, he reached around and unlocked the door. "It's cold. You should go in."

Yes, she should. She really should.

Though wishing they had more time together to talk about deeper subjects, tonight was not the time. She started to turn away, but Rio pulled her back.

Her pulse leaped at his expression. In the shadowy moonlight, he seemed to search her face for answers to questions he couldn't ask, as if he struggled with something he wanted to share but couldn't.

A heavy, hurting vibe pulsed from him, and Eden's heart ached in return.

"Rio?" she questioned, giving him an opening.

With a resigned sigh, he shook his head then kissed her cheek. His voice a whisper against her skin, he said, "Goodnight, Eden."

He reached for his crutches but Eden stopped him with a hand to his jacketed arm. "Rio, wait."

He did. And before she could think through the decision, Eden pulled his face down to hers and kissed him for real. Short, sweet, but with enough emotion for him to get the message.

Matching his words, she whispered, "Goodnight, Rio. Thank you."

Then she slipped inside and watched from a window as he hobbled to his car and drove away.

She didn't even remember to turn on the Christmas lights.

Chapter Thirteen

Tonight had to be the end. He wouldn't see her again.

Not even for the veterans' party on Saturday.

Those were the lies Rio told himself as he drifted off to sleep, only to relive the entire evening with Eden in his dreams.

Except, in the dream, she wore a headband of reindeer antlers.

He awoke with a smile on his face.

For a few pleasant minutes, he let his thoughts drift. He couldn't remember a night he'd enjoyed more. So much so that he'd almost told her the truth about his life. Somehow his training had kicked in and he'd managed to turn away.

It wasn't that he didn't trust her. He did, a real shocker. He, who hadn't trusted anyone since he was twelve years old, knew Eden would keep any secret he told her. The problem wasn't trust. The problem was the revulsion on her face if she knew.

Last night, he simply couldn't bear to see it.

Then, while he'd battled himself, she'd kissed him. No matter how brief, or how many kisses he'd experienced with other women, that one was special. In those too-short seconds, her heart had spoken to his and he'd felt something he'd not felt since before his mother died. Loved.

In the brief joining of her lips to his, Eden had transmitted a pure, unselfish love that asked for nothing but gave everything.

She was all the treasure a good man could want. Trouble was, he was not a good man. And he didn't want anything to hurt Eden, least of all him.

What was he going to do about his Mary Sunshine?

The question drove away the pleasant cloud he'd been floating on while half awake.

He'd come to Oklahoma on a mission. Two, actually. Last night, he'd accomplished one. JP was married and off for a brief honeymoon.

The only thing left for Rio to do was to force his dad into a showdown. He didn't know if that was possible, but he had to make the attempt.

After shooting off another congratulatory text to JP, offering a rain check to Brandt's invitation to lunch and, laughing in spite of himself at a funny text from Eden of dogs barking "Jingle-Bells," he dressed and drove the hour and a half to the prison where his dad had spent the past twenty years.

Because of him.

The huge gray complex before him looked bleak and lifeless beneath the sunless winter day. As he passed through the security gates a heavy dread settled in his gut.

Right now, he wanted to believe in prayer the way Eden did.

For some reason, probably her again, he heard himself mutter, "God, if You're real, convince my dad to see me."

With a shake of his head, he scoffed. His dad was the one who'd taught him that there was no higher power than himself.

Yet, the brilliant scientist who'd given him life and taught him that God and everything to do with religion was a myth for weak people now resided inside these walls of razor-wire tops and guard towers.

Rio's authoritarian father was no longer in control of anything, certainly not his own destiny.

Except for his rejection of his only son.

Rio parked in the visitors' parking area and pushed through the sharp wind toward the entrance. His crutches made tapping sounds on the endless concrete. Iron-clad security surrounded the building, intentionally obvious.

He hadn't been here since he was eighteen, about to leave for the military but trying one more time to understand what had happened and why. If anything, the place looked more austere.

After going through yet more security checks and leaving his cell phone, keys, wallet and crutches, Rio was taken to the visitation room to wait. The place smelled like human sweat and the worst disinfectant available.

Somewhere, metal clanged above the constant clamor of male voices. An alarm sounded and the guard glanced toward the adjacent hallway as a door automatically slammed shut. With a bored expression, he said to Rio, "Probably a fight. You're safe."

Rio almost rolled his eyes. He was safer here than most of the places he'd lived since the last time he'd sat and waited for a dad who refused to see him.

Would today be the same?

He'd called ahead. Felt hopeful when the receptionist agreed to the impromptu visit. "Prisoner Hendrix doesn't get many visitors. None this year. And it's Christmas."

She sounded sad, as if every prisoner should have visitors during the bogus holidays.

Except, Christmas didn't seem so bogus lately.

After a two-hour wait, another guard, this one built like a brick wall, came toward him. "You Prisoner Hendrix's son?"

Rio stood, ignoring the ache in his left leg. "Yes, sir. I'm Rio Hendrix."

"Come with me. Warden wants to see you."

Not wanting to jump to conclusions, Rio nonetheless had a moment of uncharacteristic concern. "Is my dad all right?"

Terrible how a man could both love and hate his own father.

"Far as I know."

That didn't tell him much, but in minutes he was showed into the warden's office where an older, balding man in a business suit sat behind an industrial-looking desk in a plain room with bars on the windows.

No cushy suite for this warden. Rio respected that.

The guard made a quick introduction and stepped outside the door. To wait for him, Rio supposed. An escort.

The warden waved him into a chair. "Mr. Hendrix, your father has refused to see you for twenty years. What made you think today would be any different?"

A positive-energy elf. A bright spot in his dark life. Hope.

Or stubborn stupidity.

"I've been out of country for a few years. Thought I'd try again."

"Guard said you've been waiting for hours."

"I'll wait longer if he'll talk to me."

"He won't."

Though he'd been prepared for the rejection, the warden's blunt words hit him like a blow. He swallowed the hurt. "I figured as much."

"Yet you regularly post money to his prison account."

Rio shrugged. "Auto withdrawal. He can't refuse it like he does my letters and calls. Tell me how he is. How he spends his days. If he ever talks about his family. About me? Or my mother?"

The warden heaved a massive sigh. "All I can tell you is that he is alive and well. Sorry for the wasted trip."

The cloud of doom, hovering before, settled on

him as heavy as boulders. He'd told himself not to get his hopes up. But he had.

Still, he felt as bereft and, yes, as guilty, as he had the day officers had taken his only remaining parent, shackled and silent, from the courtroom for the trip to life in prison.

That day, Rio had become a social orphan, a ward of the system that had convicted his father of first-degree murder.

Withdrawing an envelope from his jacket, Rio laid it on the desk. There was nothing left for him to do. "Give this to him. If he refuses, toss it in the trash."

He couldn't knowingly take another rejection.

Fueled by joy and renewed holiday spirit from last night's beautiful wedding, Eden barely noticed the fatigue from her long day of dog grooming. Time was running out before Saturday's party and she had tons of gifts to wrap. Gift wrapping was fun, and a certain non-Christmas lover had volunteered to help. She hoped he remembered.

If not, she was about to jog his mind.

Eden slid one final box of gifts into the back of her Escape. Then, hurrying to the back door of her home, she leaned inside and yelled, "I'm leaving, Grandpa. Text if you need me."

"Will do."

Satisfied he and Mom, whom she'd visited early this morning to share breakfast, were okay, Eden slammed her cargo hatch.

"Load up, Brinkley. Let's go see Rio."

The jingle bells on his collar chiming, her little buddy leaped into the vehicle and settled in his spot in the passenger seat. After buckling him in, they were off, with Christmas carols filling the car and stoking her joy.

The hotel, which reminded Eden too much of Rio's temporary status, was a short drive. Stopping at the ice cream store to grab some goodies, she tried not to overbuy. Hotel fridges were painfully small. But both she and Rio loved ice cream, especially in winter.

She liked that they shared this one oddball preference.

At the hotel, she loaded her arms with as many bags as she could manage, hooked Brinkley's leash to her wrist and took the elevator up to his door.

She knocked. "Room service."

From inside, she heard movement, and then the door opened.

"I didn't order room—" Rio's words drifted to a stop. Hair mussed, countenance grim, he looked like the end of hard times.

Eden held up the ice cream bag. "I bring Christmas cheer, gifts to wrap and chocolate ice cream. With fudge sauce."

Rio scraped a hand through his unruly hair. "Look, Eden, I'm not…uh…this isn't a good time. I don't feel so great."

"Are you sick?" She stepped around him to place

the bags on the floor. "Can I get you anything? Aspirin? Flu medicine? Gatorade?"

Still holding the door open, he pivoted on his one good foot. "No."

That was it? Just no.

"Do you have fever?" She placed the back of her hand against his forehead.

Rio backed away from her. "No."

She cocked her head. "So, you're not sick?"

"No."

"Is that the only word you can utter today?"

Instead of the humor she expected, he sighed and rubbed a hand down his beard. He still hadn't closed the door.

"Well, something is definitely wrong. Right?" She couldn't even grin at her silly phrasing. Rio was hurting, though not from his broken bone or from sickness.

Eden reached around him and shut the door. He was a friend in need—a lot more than a friend, actually—and he was painfully alone. She would be remiss if she didn't try to help.

Eden was the last person he should see right now, but she was the only one he wanted. Talk about a messed-up head. Rio felt about as dark as the biggest black hole in the universe. She had no business anywhere near him.

"I'm not good company today." Or, for her, any other day.

"Did something happen?" As if she'd had a sudden realization, Eden's eyes widened. "Did you reinjure your leg?"

"The leg is fine."

Brinkley, the emotion-sensitive dog, tugged against his leash toward Rio. Eden unsnapped him, and sure enough, the pup trotted to him, black button eyes sympathetic.

He didn't even deserve the kindness of a dog, much less from a beautiful spirit like Eden.

As he'd brooded over the failed visit to the prison, he'd come to a realization. For his dad to endlessly reject him, he must have been wrong about what he'd seen and heard that awful day when his mother died. He'd been so certain. Now, he wasn't.

"You should go, Eden. Nothing for you here."

She stopped rattling the Braum's sack to stare at him.

He didn't want to hurt her. That's all he was capable of. Hurting the people he loved. And while she stood there in her Santa hat and ugly Christmas sweater with a carton of ice cream in one hand and compassion in her eyes, Rio faced the truth. He loved her. Which meant she really, really, needed to get away from him as fast as possible.

"What's wrong, Rio? Talk to me. Please. Whatever is going on behind those gorgeous eyes of yours hurts you. And that hurts me."

He closed the eyes she admired and wished he could be the kind of man she deserved.

"Come over here." She took his arm and led him to the table. For once, she didn't insist he use the crutches. Nor did he refuse her leading, though he should have.

"Sit," she said. "I'll make fudge sundaes and we'll talk. Then, if you're up to it, we'll wrap these gifts for Saturday."

Though he wanted to pour his heart out, Rio let his training kick in. *Never confess. Never get personally involved. Stick to the mission.*

He remained standing, stiff and gritty. "I mean it, Eden. You should go."

"I'm not leaving you alone to brood. Something is wrong, and I want to help. Did you get bad news about your job situation?"

Rio emitted a half groan, half growl, battling to stay focused on anything but her and the hunger in him to let her in. "You're frustrating me."

"I don't mean to. I'm sorry. It's just that you keep so much inside—which isn't healthy, by the way." She touched his cheek, and he was catapulted to last night and the way she'd rocked his world.

It was all he could do not to pull her into his arms and pour out every hurt and heartache. To declare that he loved her and would do anything to keep her in his life.

Neither of which he dared do.

Keeping her safe was more important.

She needed to leave. Right now.

Yet he didn't move and she went on talking.

"Everyone needs someone else to lean on once in a while, Rio. Even strong, tough, really smart guys like you. The Bible says sharing the load makes it lighter. Did you know that?"

No, he didn't.

"Psychologists too," she said. "I'm small but I'm strong. Remember?"

Yes, he remembered the way she'd lifted the Harley that first, fateful day when they'd met.

She'd impressed him then. Today, she was killing him.

If she stuck around much longer, he'd break. His greatest tortures—love and compassion—would strip away years of mental training. From the only woman who'd ever touched his soul. A woman with an inner light of goodness who had no business even crossing into his shadow.

An interior battle raged in Rio to keep her close or to drive her away. Finally, his superior brain overruled his heart. A cruel word was the only way to end this before it was too late. And Rio knew how to be cruel. He knew how to punch at the most vulnerable spot.

Through clenched teeth, he ground out in his harshest tone, "Can't you get it through your Christmas-warped brain that I don't want you here? Take your Jesus and your ice cream and your Good Samaritan dog and get out!"

Eden dropped his arm. Her joyful light dimmed. Brinkley abandoned him to whine upward at his owner.

"Okay." The word came out in a whisper. She picked up the ice cream container, but instead of replacing it in the sack, she stuck the carton inside the small fridge. Wounded brown eyes tried to smile. "Maybe you'll want it later. To make you feel better."

If she'd screamed at him or thrown the ice cream carton, he'd have been okay. But for reasons Rio didn't try to understand, the kind word and the gifted ice cream ripped away his defenses.

He collapsed on the hotel chair and thrust his head in his hands.

"You have to go," he groaned, "but I don't want you to."

"I'm not leaving." She settled next to him on the chair arm, her small hand on his bowed back. He couldn't hear her words but she was murmuring something, and Rio suspected she was praying. For him.

Even if prayer was useless, *her* belief that prayer made a difference gave Rio a strange kind of hope.

He'd left all *his* hope behind at the prison, so Eden must have brought it in with her. Either that, or God was real.

Eyes on the floor and the little dog who seemed as determined as Eden to offer comfort, Rio said, "I'm not a good man, Eden."

"That's not true."

"Yes, it is." He straightened, determined to make her see who he really was. It was the only way to keep her safe. "I've done things that would shock you, bad things. For good reasons, but they're still bad. I've done things for the cause of freedom that

I can never share with anyone. You deserve better than that. Better than me."

"You can't blame yourself for what you had to do in the military."

"I'm not talking about the Rangers, Eden. Oh, that was bad enough. I'm referencing my current employment for the US government. Highly classified, ugly business Uncle Sam pretends doesn't happen."

"Is that supposed to upset me? Because it doesn't. I'd already figured out that your work involved things you couldn't discuss. Your job doesn't make you a terrible person. It makes you a man who cares about this country and freedom around the world. Someone standing up against evil. I think you're pretty special."

His mouth twisted in derision. "Right."

If only she knew...and he was very glad she didn't.

"You listen to me, Rio Hendrix. You're kind, unselfish, incredibly smart and brave." She showed him her dimples. "And really fun to dance with."

Did she have any idea how much he wanted to believe her? And how much danger she was in if he did?

He knew better. She didn't. Only his enemies knew the lengths to which he'd go in pursuit of the greater good. The way he had since he was a boy standing up against his own father. Although it had been too late by then. The damage had been done. His mother was dead.

His mother. His father. The other truth Eden didn't know, and the only remaining weapon that could open her eyes to the real Rio Hendrix.

Bolting up from the couch, he moved away. Eden's nearness muddled his brain.

"I'm a great actor, Eden. It's what I do for a living. I play a role, pretend to be someone I'm not in pursuit of my government's goals. I'm good at it. I am not any of those things you say. It's all been an act, a means to an end."

Although he could not say what his goal had been this time.

"I don't believe you." Eden's calm denial stoked his desperation. For an intelligent woman, she was stubbornly blind to the faults of others. Him, especially.

One last shot to open her eyes.

Saying the words would rip his heart in two. But he had to. For her sake.

"Then believe this. My dad is in prison." He pounded a fist against his chest. "My testimony sent him there. Me, a twelve-year-old kid, sat on the witness stand and swore that my own father murdered my mother. A murderer, Eden. That's who I come from. That's who I am. I put my own father in prison for life. And I carry his murderous DNA." He dropped his head, blew out a breath, heard the pounding in his ears. "From that point on, there was nowhere left for me to go but down."

He expected her to be repulsed. He wanted her to be.

She wasn't. Instead, her next words melted an icy place inside him. "Oh, Rio. I am so sorry. How horrible for you. No child should ever go through that. Twelve years old. You were only a boy."

"Yeah, well, that's what I got for thinking I'm so smart. The prosecution claimed my IQ and exceptional memory made me a responsible witness."

A memory that gave him fits at times. There were some things he'd like to forget but couldn't.

"And I'm sure you were," she said.

"I'm not sure at all. I was a kid. What if I was wrong? That's what the defense lawyers said. They claimed I was a mixed-up, traumatized kid who already hated my father."

"Is that true? Were you confused?"

"I don't know. I don't think so. I hated what my father did, but I don't think I hated *him*." Not then, anyway.

"Were there other witnesses?"

"A few. People who knew my dad could be controlling. The usual expert witnesses, my mother's coworkers, Dad's boss."

"They all testified against him?"

"Yes." The DA had built a case of a brilliant, coldhearted, dictatorial narcissist with little respect for human life. That, along with Rio's testimony, had sealed Professor Carlton Hendrix's fate. And Rio's. "None of that matters, Eden. I was the star witness. My testimony put him in prison."

Eden rose and came to him. She slid both arms around his waist and pinned him with her soft, understanding gaze. "You think that makes you a terrible man? It doesn't."

"Didn't you hear everything I just said?"

"Neither your father's crime, nor your job, form your identity. From where I'm standing, you're incredible. You did the right thing even when it hurt you."

"Sorry. Don't see it." Oh, but he wanted to. He wanted to see himself through her eyes.

"I do, and news flash. I'm the one looking. You can't see yourself."

Her spunky reasoning brought a half-hearted snort.

"And guess what?" she went on. "I see what you don't. Regardless of a broken bone and a heavy heart and apparently a ton of worry, you've gone out of your way for me and a building full of lonely old veterans."

"That's no big deal. I owe them. And I like hanging out with you."

She flashed a smiled at the last. "I like hanging out with you, too. To those veterans, your company is a big deal. Everyone in this country and half the world owes them, but you take the time to appreciate the people they still are."

"So do you."

"They relate to you in a way they never have to me. Oh, they like me, and they love Brinkley, but they *relate* to you. Did you know skin-and-bones Ed Frazer has gained weight and stopped fighting the nurses since you arrived?"

He didn't. "All we do is play chess after he finishes lunch."

"A lunch he barely touched until you started eating with him. Almost daily, I'm told. The nurse says he's also asking for extra Ensure and snacks in order to, and I quote, 'Sharpen up his gray matter so he can beat you in chess.' He even asked her to order a chess mastery book from Amazon."

"Old guy was furious the first time we played and I let him win. Tried to punch me. Said it was insulting." Rio shook his head, warmed by the memory. "He was right. I don't do that anymore."

"See what I mean. Only a thoughtful man would recognize the insult."

"That's not altruism. I like to play chess, and Ed's decent competition."

"What about my grandpa? You make his day whenever you stop for coffee and conversation."

"Steven's a great guy."

"So are you. Without your ideas and expertise, we wouldn't have raised the money for Saturday's big party. I needed fresh ideas and another hand, and you stepped up." Her sweet-tasting lips curved. "Which isn't easy on one foot."

The temptation rose to press a kiss against that smile. Rio resisted. Barely.

Eden was like a magnet to his will of iron. He wouldn't kiss her again, but he could touch her, hold her—loosely, as he must everything and everyone.

"You have a knack, you know."

"For what?" Shining brown eyes searched his.

Could she read the love he tried to hide? The longing to believe he was even half of what she said?

"Finding the positive."

"Oh, that's easy. The Bible says to focus on whatever is true, noble and just. I see all three of those in you."

True, noble, just, lovely, of good report. His brain had inadvertently memorized the poster hanging in her salon. For Eden, the verse wasn't only a saying. She lived by it.

She was all of those things and more. The effervescent one. The beaming ray of sunlight breaking through his darkness.

Oh, yes, he loved her. A fool's game he'd never played and one he could not win. Nor could she, no matter how many positive vibes she exuded.

He needed to get away, and yet, one tiny elf kept him glued to the floor.

"When my dad was killed," she said, "my mother told me something that I live by. She said we could either let anger and bitterness destroy us or we could let God heal our grief and cling to Him and celebrate the amazing man Dad was."

Her dad, a warrior like him, who'd sacrificed the ultimate to make the world better, safer. Yet, it wasn't. "How old were you when he died?"

"Twelve."

Twelve. The same age as he was when his mother was murdered.

Ridiculous how he'd once thought Eden had never had a care in her life.

"Losing a parent at the same age," he muttered. "Not a great thing to have in common."

"I agree. The way they died, at the hands of someone else, is crushing and unjust. But God remains faithful, and someday He'll right all the wrongs and heal all the hurts."

Rio surprised himself by saying, "I hope you're right."

"I am." Her expression softened. "Because of Jesus, I know there is good in this world, in people like you, and all those who are making Saturday's party the best ever. There are beautiful, wonderful things to appreciate and enjoy. All we have to do is look around."

At the lilt in her tone, her little dog leaped up and spun in a circle. His collar bells jingled.

"Like dogs?" he asked, amused. She did that for him. Lifted his gloom and amused him.

"Dogs are some of the best!" With a happy laugh, Eden crouched on her toes to rub Brinkley's ears.

"Right up there with ice cream, I suppose?"

"Yes. But right below Christmas." She aimed a pointed look toward the small round table. "Which reminds me, where is your tree?"

To relieve his aching leg, Rio limped to the easy chair. "Maid must have taken it."

He hadn't lied. Housekeeping emptied the trash can every day.

Eden waved off the concern. "I'll bring you another one."

"Forget about it."

"You still have your Santa hat and headbands, though, right?"

"Well..." He hedged. "The maid might have picked those up, too."

Suspicion narrowed her eyes. "You rat. You tossed them, didn't you?"

At that point, he gave up and chuckled, guilty.

Even though she was probably aggravated, Eden laughed with him. Right before she punched him in the arm.

"Featherweight," he said.

And they both laughed some more.

The mood in the room, heavy and somber before, had lifted like morning fog. The problems were still there. His dad still hated him. He still didn't know if his testimony had been true. And he still had blood on his hands. An ocean of blood. Yet the horrible ache in his gut and the mental torment had dissipated.

Because of her.

"Please understand, Rio, that I'm not making light of the things you've told me. I won't insult you by saying I understand everything you feel. That's not possible. But I'm here for you. I care about you. No matter what you say, I'm convinced you're a good man doing what he believes is right regardless of the great cost to himself."

How could a man fight against a woman who refused to see anything but the positive? He couldn't.

He was a master at reading people. Eden more than cared. She was falling in love with him.

The terrifying truth was that he'd already fallen. He wanted her in his life with a ferocity usually reserved for warfare. Yet her lifestyle and his didn't match. He had terrorists to stop. She had dogs to groom.

The gulf between them was too wide to span.

No matter what she said, or how either of them felt, they were vastly different.

Soon, he would be far, far away from Rosemary Ridge. And Eden Carnegie.

For her sake, soon needed to come tomorrow.

Chapter Fourteen

Eden sat across the breakfast table from her grandpa, savoring the pancakes and bacon he'd prepared and insisted she eat before starting her day at the salon.

Not that she'd argued. She loved buttermilk pancakes.

"Would you mind wrapping a few gifts today?" she asked around a syrupy bite.

"Don't mind at all. You still have a lot?"

"I dropped some packages off with Rachel. She's going to share them around and get them wrapped, but I still have quite a few left."

"Thought you and Rio were doing that last night."

"I'd planned to but—" She lay her fork aside and took a sip of coffee. "Grandpa, what do you think of him?"

"Rio? Well, he's a smart guy." Grandpa toasted her with his coffee cup and a grin. "Seems taken with you."

"I like him, too, but he's not a Christian." She toyed with a broken piece of bacon. "You know my beliefs on the subject. I want someone who shares my faith."

"He and I've done some talking about that."

Surprised, she asked, "You have? Was he receptive?"

"He's a good listener. But poker-faced. Doesn't reveal much."

"He's had a hard life."

"Yes, he has, Eden, and you have a tender heart. I don't want you getting hurt."

Eden nibbled on the bit of bacon. She didn't want that, either, but she thought Grandpa's warning may have come too late.

She finished her breakfast and made her way across the backyard toward her salon and the first morning client.

Lucky the boxer and his owner came through the gate next to the street. Brinkley trotted over to greet him.

The two touched noses and did their usual sniffing while Eden discussed Lucky's training progress with the owner. "Have you taken him downtown since our last class?"

"Yes, and he did great. No tugging, and he completely ignored the traffic."

"Awesome, Shirley. I won't have time to take him into town today, but I'll test him on everything else. If he passes like I think he will, this should be our last session."

"You're a marvel. No wonder you have a waiting list."

Eden smiled. The waiting list was something she hoped to shorten very soon. Once the Christmas party was over and paid for, she would no longer need to spend hours before opening the shop training and walking dogs.

Even though she'd enjoyed the tasks, she was tired and ready for a break.

"Lucky's a great dog. Plus, you've followed every bit of advice I've given you. Owner compliance is key to success."

"Thank you, Eden." The woman handed over Lucky's leash and left.

An hour later, as Eden finished with Lucky and turned him over to his owner, she glimpsed a sleek black sports car passing on the street.

Her pulse jittered. Was it Rio?

Last night had been both heartrending and wonderful. Rio had opened up to her, and though she'd ached to learn of his painful past, she'd felt special that he'd trusted her. Over ice cream sundaes, he'd admitted that he'd never told those things to another soul and asked her to keep his confidence.

She would.

While she prayed for his broken soul to heal, she'd ask God to open his father's heart, too. Rio needed to see the man and find closure. Or a renewed relationship. She prayed for some of both.

A car door slammed on the street, but, after a minute, Rio didn't appear at the gate.

"Must have been another black car," she muttered to Brinkley, admittedly disappointed.

Then she went inside the salon to begin the day, aware that every thought and prayer would be about Rio Hendrix.

Rio resisted the urge to cross into the back yard and spend the morning with Eden. It wouldn't be the first time he'd watched her work and listened to her cheerful chatter. He loved being in her sunny presence.

This morning, however, he'd come to see her grandfather. He'd even brought doughnuts.

As if he wasn't surprised by the visit, Steven, dragging his oxygen tubing, waved Rio into the house. "I hear you kids had a great time at the wedding the other night."

Eden apparently had kept her promise so far and said nothing about last night's uncharacteristic revelations. The cynic in him had awakened this morning worried that she had. And more worried that she'd come to her senses and tell him to get lost.

He'd do that soon enough. She needn't bother.

"Nice wedding," he said. "Did she tell you about the dance? Or anything else I should know?"

Steven's laugh ended on a cough. "Taffy sent over some pictures and a video."

He'd have to confiscate those. Get them scrubbed. Make sure they never appeared anywhere public.

The internet was dangerous to a man who had to remain invisible from the rest of the world.

The thought made him tired. Always fighting the good fight, always hiding, could grow wearisome, even to him. Until lately, he'd liked the challenge of his work and figured he would again once he heard from his bosses. Unless they booted him out of a career for something he hadn't done. When Uncle Sam couldn't learn the culprit, they dismissed everyone involved.

The thought gave him indigestion. And he was out of Tums.

Steven eyed his boot cast. "Where's your crutches?"

"In the car. Don't need them much anymore." Anyway, that was Rio's diagnosis. The leg ached a little if he remained standing long. Otherwise, he was good to go. Ready for assignment. He'd see the doc again this afternoon to verify the hopeful sign he'd gotten at the last appointment. One way or the other, he was dumping the crutches, maybe the boot.

"Brought doughnuts." He raised the white sack. "Got any coffee?"

"Always."

Rio followed the older man into the old-fashioned eat-in kitchen and plunked the bag on the table. "I smell bacon. You've already eaten."

"Eden got up early. Had a training class." Steven went to the coffee maker, took cups from a small stand, and poured the brew. "Can't have her working all day on an empty stomach. Half the time, she won't stop for lunch."

"Busy time of year." Rio retrieved both mugs and placed them on the table.

"That's what she says." With a relieved exhale, Steven settled into a chair. "What brings you out this morning? Come to see my pretty granddaughter? She'll be in the shop by now."

Ignoring the question and the leap in his belly at the thought of seeing her later, Rio sipped the steaming drink. Robust, black, the way he'd learned out of necessity to enjoy it in Turkey. Minus the Turkish coffee grounds. "Wanted to talk to you about something."

The former lawman eyed Rio as if gauging his intent.

"Okay. Shoot."

"Getting to know you and Eden has caused me to rethink some things. JP and Brandt, too. JP's become a regular evangelist."

"Ah. I see. You're asking about our faith in Jesus."

Steven had always been astute. The trait had made him a great cop.

"I suppose. In a way." Searching for the right words, Rio opened the white bag and removed a warm doughnut. Chocolate iced, which reminded him of Eden and the fudgy ice cream they'd finally eaten last night after he'd spilled his guts and admitted his shame. That she hadn't been repulsed still amazed and impressed him.

Steven eyed him over a coffee cup. "You have questions?"

"Yes." Too many. "One big one." He bit into the doughnut and chewed.

Steven waved toward the bag. "Give me one of those."

Rio's mouth quirked. "I thought you'd had breakfast."

"I have, but there's always room for a doughnut. Mostly air anyway." With a chuckle, he patted his round belly. "Don't be stingy."

With an answering chuckle, Rio pushed the bag across the table and they ate in comfortable silence for a couple of minutes.

Steven finished one doughnut and reached for another. "Better start talking before I polish off the whole sack in anticipation."

Rio went to the sink and ripped off two paper towels, dropped one next to Steven and wiped his hands and mouth with the other.

He wasn't sure where to begin.

"Eden's the most positive person I've ever met."

"Can't disagree. I'm proud of her. Good girl. Loves Jesus."

Good girl who loves Jesus, both of which gave Rio fits.

"I don't understand how anyone believes in a good God."

"What do you mean?"

"As a cop, you've seen evil firsthand. So have I. God, if He exists, can't be benevolent, or He wouldn't let those things happen."

"So—" a thoughtful Steven laid his half-eaten doughnut aside "—are you asking if God exists? Or why He lets bad things happen?"

"Both, I guess."

"Well, son, the first one's easy. God exists. You

see Him everywhere if you look. My granddaughter. The change in your buddies. The innocence of a child. In nature's beauty. Music. In answered prayer, of which I've had plenty."

"What about wars? Murders?" He kept his face passive but the word *murder* always generated horrific images of his mother that he couldn't forget. "Abuse? Crime? Eden's dad dying in the Middle East. Her mother's dementia. Where is God in any of that?"

If God was real and cared, why had Rio and others like him spent their lives fighting an unwinnable war against evil? All they or anyone else had ever managed was to stem the tide for a short while.

He'd begun to wonder if the effort was worth the cost. Or if God was playing a cosmic joke on all of the fools He'd created.

Steven folded his fleshy arms on the tabletop. "I'm no theologian, but a few things I do know. God created us for relationship with Him. He didn't want robots or puppets, so he gave us a free will. Choices. To do right or to do wrong. Good or evil. We get to make the decision. If we're smart, we choose according to the standards He gave us to live by."

"Then humans must be idiots."

"We live in a fallen world. Evil, disasters, disease, are never God's will or His plan for humanity. That's why He sent Jesus. To give us hope and show us a better way."

The old cop sounded like JP.

"I thought religion was a fantasy for the weak." Thanks to a father who'd drilled the concept deep into his mind from the time he was four and reading science articles. Science and human intellect reigned supreme. Nothing else existed.

"How has that belief worked out for you, son?"

Steven's quiet, gentle words swirled around inside Rio's head. Most of his life, he'd believed only in himself. He'd been confident in who he was, in what his brain and body could accomplish. Still was, if intellect and skill were the topics.

But in believing his father's one-sided view, he'd ignored the voice inside that had gotten louder over the years and become a megaphone since his arrival in Rosemary Ridge.

From the books JP had loaned him, he'd begun to see things differently.

There was more to a person than his head. There was his heart. And his soul, the portion of humanity undefinable by mathematical calculations or scientific inquiry.

No matter how he or his dad had denied its existence, it was there, inside him. Except in his case, the soul was dark and empty.

He yearned for something he could no longer explain away.

The door of Eden's grooming salon swept open while she wrestled a handsome black Lab into a harness. Or tried to. Jett was having none of it today. The Lab wasn't a biter, but he was big, strong and reluctant.

"Need some help?" Rio's deep voice sounded amused.

"Jett hates having his nails clipped, but I can handle him." Eventually, she always won.

As if to prove her wrong, the Labrador wrenched free and leaped to the floor before she could slide the restraint into place.

He plopped on his bottom and glared at her, deeply affronted.

Eden glanced from the stubborn dog to the man. Rio's eyes twinkled. He held out his palm toward the dog.

Jett, the traitor, offered him a paw.

"Weren't you the one who told me that two were better than one?" Rio asked. "Because we all need help now and then. Yada yada."

"Yada yada is right. I see you're without the crutches. Good news?"

"Told you I'm a fast healer."

His news relieved a smidgen of her guilt at being the reason he'd suffered through several weeks on one foot.

She reached down to rub Jett's floppy ears. He tilted his head into her hand. "He's a nice dog; he just hates anyone to restrain him long enough for a trim."

"Want him back on the table?"

"Yes." Before she could slide her arms under Jett and do the task, Rio lifted him up and held him in place. Jett hunkered down and whined in protest of the betrayal.

Rio stroked the dog's ears. "What's next?"

"Keep rubbing his ears and feed him this treat while I slip on the harness and snap the restraint." She indicated the overhead leash she used to maintain control.

"No muzzle?"

"Once the harness is in place, he knows he's caught and he'll cooperate. Reluctantly." She flashed a smile. "I'm really happy about your leg."

"That makes two of us. I'll be back on my Harley soon, if JP hasn't auctioned it off."

Aware that he'd stored his bike in Zoey's garage, Eden snickered and got down to the business of dog grooming.

They worked together, with Rio soothing the dog with rubs and treats while Eden clipped the canine nails.

She was inordinately happy to have Rio stop by and not because of his timely assistance. They talked as she worked but neither mentioned last night's confessions.

"Had coffee with your grandpa."

"That's nice of you." Grandpa's day had been made. He loved company. "After all his years as a public servant, he gets lonely for people. When he's feeling decent, which isn't often these days, he goes to the senior center for a few hours. Church helps, too."

"That's what we talked about."

Her heart leaped. "Church?"

"Religion. Your faith. Good and evil."

Eden held her breath, wondering how to respond. She didn't want to push but was thrilled that he was thinking about the single most important topic in the world.

As she began to clean Jett's ears, she asked, "What brought that on?"

Rio picked up the slicker brush she'd laid on the table and stroked it over Jett's back. "You have something I don't. Even with chaos and problems all around, you seem peaceful."

"I am. God's got me."

"You believe it and you live it. That impresses me."

"Because it's true. I know you struggle with accepting that God is real and that He cares, but I *know* what I know." She tapped two fingers over her heart. "In here, I know."

"Frankly, I hadn't give God much thought until you broke my leg."

Eden saw the glint of humor in his face and dimpled. "See how God brings good out of something bad?"

She was teasing, too, but only halfway.

"I'm starting to." Rio followed the slicker brush with a palm over Jett's smooth coat. "JP gave me a couple of C. S. Lewis books and another detailing the historical and theological proof that Jesus is Who you say He is. Fascinating, factual evidence."

Her pulse executed a hard thump. Hope ballooned in her chest. "And?"

Rio paused in brushing, voice low and contemplative. "If Jesus is true, then God is also real. Otherwise, why do human beings exist? Why are we here? And why is this life so short and our understanding so limited? There must be more. The natural universe points to intelligent design, perhaps driven by evolutionary phenomena, perhaps not. I'm still contemplating how that all works together. Either way, the evidence for God's existence overwhelms my doubts."

Eden pressed her lips together to suppress a laugh. Rio's brain had outdistanced her. "What does all that even mean?"

"Simply put, I believe in your Jesus. Otherwise life has no meaning."

Throat tight with emotion, Eden wanted to jump around the room and shout praises. Instead, she said, "Rio, that's the best Christmas present I've ever had. I could just hug you."

He dropped the slicker brush and came around the table to where she stood.

"I think we can do better than that." Expression tender, eyes alight with newfound faith, he took her in his arms and, while her heart pounded out of her chest and the dogs looked on, pressed his lips to hers.

The smile they shared was as powerful as the kiss.

Almost.

Chapter Fifteen

Rio preferred to spend the rest of the day celebrating his inexplicable lightheartedness with the effervescent one, who knew a thing or two about joy. Instead, he drove to the physician's clinic for the scheduled checkup on his broken bones. With the news that the weight-bearing bone was healed well enough to ditch the crutches and wear only the boot, since he was doing that anyway, he considered today a good day. A real good day.

He couldn't quite understand what had changed. All he'd done was admit that he believed in Jesus, but he felt different, lighter, and as if he was hungry for a food he'd never tasted.

"Weird," he said to his steering wheel. Had he gone over the edge? Or discovered the missing link in his life?

Either way, he wasn't going to fight the swarm of good emotions. They didn't happen that often. Never, actually, in this manner.

Aiming the car toward his Harley and Brandt at the House of Hope, he passed his hotel and the business with the inflatable Christmas figures.

They still annoyed him, but not for his previous reasons. Lopsided or collapsed on the ground, they just looked silly.

However, the big Christmas tree at the town center and the lighted gazebo in the park didn't annoy him at all. And the life-sized nativity scene of the Holy Family outside a church filled his chest with gratitude and awe. He stopped in the parking lot for a few minutes to admire the display and did something he'd never done in his life. He prayed. For real.

Pouring out his past and all the things he'd done that weighed on his mind and darkened his soul, he asked God to help him be more like Eden. Not that he could ever be anywhere near as godly, but he could do better than he was.

For a long while, he remained parked in front of the nativity scene, pondering his newfound faith and the surrounding beauty he'd never given much notice. Wispy white cirrus clouds drifted across a deep blue sky. The rich, varied greens of pine and cedar, holly and boxwood broke the monotony of winter's brown. A flash of red caught his attention as a cardinal lighted on the church railing.

Like Steven said, God was all around. All he'd had to do was look and believe.

Christmas was a great time to do exactly that.

His phone tweeted. Rio rubbed a hand over his face, shocked to feel moisture. He never cried. He fought. Outsmarted. Tricked. But he didn't cry. Hadn't since he was twelve years old.

With humor, he muttered, "I hope this isn't the start of something, God."

And then he read Brandt's text.

Still coming over?

Rio texted back.

On my way now. Break out the confetti. I have news.

Brandt replied with a confetti emoji and a row of question marks.

Rio tossed the phone onto the bucket seat, wished Eden was sitting there, and pulled out of the lot.

As if she was in the Mustang with him, he switched on the radio and turned the dial to Christmas music. This time of year, sounds of the season weren't hard to find.

"Feliz Navidad" came on. He recalled the night Eden had challenged him to sing along in Spanish. Today he did.

By the time the song ended and "Mary, Did You Know?" came on, he parked the sports car along the curb outside the House of Hope. He was going to miss this car when he returned it to the rental place. He'd miss these people, too.

Brandt met him at the door. Fresh from a brief assignment in Argentina, the security specialist looked tired. "What are we celebrating?"

Rio wished JP was there as well. The two men were the closest to family he had.

"The books you and JP loaned me. I read them."

One of Brandt's eyebrows went up. "And?"

"I believe it. All of it. I've been at the church just now, praying." He'd said the last with a pinch of self-consciousness.

As if unsure he'd heard correctly, Brandt searched his expression, waiting for the joke. When Rio didn't blink or budge, his friend broke into a wide grin.

"Welcome to the family." He stuck out his hand. "I thought you were going to say something different, but this is even better."

"Yeah? What were you expecting?"

"That you were going to stick around town for good and maybe marry Eden Carnegie."

Rio's gut tightened, ached.

"No." The word was harder to say than it should have been. "Can't. She's way too good for a guy like me. I never know where my job will take me."

If Uncle Sam still wanted him.

Brandt put a hand on his shoulder. "Get in here. Let's talk."

Saturday morning, the day of the Celebrate Veterans Christmas Party, Eden awoke with a smile on her face, a Christmas carol on her lips and a praise in her heart.

"Today's the day, Brinkley."

The little dog rose from his bed, stretched his paws out in front of him, and then gave a hearty shake as he smiled up at her.

When she crossed to the doggy advent calendar hanging on her bedroom wall, Brinkley trotted along, eager to discover what treat he'd receive today.

Eden opened the calendar's tiny drawer before turning the picture toward the dog. "Look, Brink, a squeaky toy."

After retrieving the actual toy from a bag on her dresser, she tossed it to him and laughed when he caught it in his teeth and gave the toy a growly tough-dog shake.

While Brinkley played, Eden dressed in black leggings, boots and a long red Christmas sweater emblazoned with one word. *Joy.* That suited her mood perfectly. After adding Mom's nativity brooch to one shoulder, she adjusted a Santa hat over her hair, dressed Brinkley in his Merry Christmas bandana and therapy dog jacket, and followed her nose to the kitchen.

"Will you come to the party this afternoon, Grandpa?" She slid onto a chair just as he placed a cup of coffee and a plate of scrambled eggs with toast in front her.

"Planning on it." He added his own plate and cup, sitting down with a heavy wheeze. "I'll take my truck, though, since you'll stay later than I want to."

Or was able to. Outings tired him quickly, but she didn't remind him of his frail health.

"I wish Mom could attend the way she used to."

Grandpa scraped butter onto his toast. "Real

shame. She loved putting on that party as much as you do."

"It was one of the things we shared in common. She was the best help. We practically read each other's minds." Scooping a cheesy bite of egg, she added, "I miss her, Grandpa, the mama she used to be."

He patted her arm. "I know you do, sis. Life is cruel sometimes. But we have a greater hope, don't we?"

She brightened. "Yes, we do, and so does Rio." She'd told him when she'd gotten home last night about the change in Rio. "I woke up this morning so thankful."

"You have strong feelings for him."

There was no longer anything to prevent her from admitting, "Everything between us has happened so fast, but yes, I do. I think I'm in love with him."

"I suspect you're not alone in that."

She offered a happy grin. "I hope you're right."

There was still the matter of his career and the secret work he did for the government. He'd said from the start that he was waiting for a call to duty and wouldn't be in town very long.

Had yesterday—and she—changed his mind?

She didn't know. She was simply glad that celebrating the veterans today took on a brighter hue because of his presence and his newfound faith.

No matter what happened, she was determined to trust God's plan. But she could hope. And pray that God's will for her included Rio Hendrix.

"Being a Christian doesn't erase all the hard things he experienced in his past, Eden." Grandpa picked up his cup and looked at her over the rim. "You need to recognize that."

"He's told me a little about his childhood."

"Did he mention how he came to be in foster care?"

"Yes." That's all she'd say about Rio's revelation, even to Grandpa. She'd promised.

"I'm aware of what happened to the boy, Eden."

Her stomach dipped. She hadn't spoken a word of Rio's confidences to anyone. Did Grandpa mean what she thought he did? That he knew about Rio's dad?

"You are? How?"

"I was a peace officer for a long time, child. Law, crime, those were my business. I followed Professor Hendrix's murder trial and his young son's part as an eyewitness. When that same boy showed up on my radar later as a teenager, I made the connection."

"You never said anything." He'd given her the recent cryptic warning to be careful, but she'd never guessed he knew about the murder. "And I've been seeing Rio nearly every day."

"The dad's crime wasn't the boy's fault. I didn't see the point in bringing up something that traumatic. Don't plan to mention it now unless he does." Grandpa paused for a few breaths. "I'll still warn you, though, to guard your heart. Rio witnessed his mother's death by his father's hand. Trauma that awful can affect a person his entire life."

"Rio's a good man. And now he's a believer."

"Not denying that. But hurt people sometimes hurt other people."

"Even after they come to know the Lord?"

"Even then. God doesn't instantly erase every wound. He just offers better tools for the healing process. Rio's a smart man, so we'll pray he takes hold of those tools."

"The story makes me so sad, Grandpa. Rio's been trying to see or talk to his dad for years, but the man refuses any contact. It torments Rio." She didn't know how to help other than to pray. "He's afraid he made a mistake. He was only a child, and even though he was a brilliant child, his dad's rejection makes him doubt his own eyes."

"Has he gone up to the prison and talked to the warden?"

"He drove up there the day after JP and Zoey's wedding." She pushed her plate away. "He was very upset that night."

"Bad deal. You cheered him up, I suppose?"

"I tried to. I listened. He talked. I don't think he does that very often. He listens more than he speaks."

Grandpa drained his coffee cup. "We better get moving. Two o'clock will be here before you know it."

Eden took her plate to the sink. "I'm sorry to leave you with the dishes again."

He waved her off. "Makes me feel useful. Go on now. You have plenty to do before the party."

She kissed his still-whiskery cheek. "Love you, Grandpa. See you there. Thanks."

With Brinkley jingling along beside her, Eden drove around town to gather last-minute items and then headed to the veterans' center. They had a party to set up.

And Rio had promised to help.

For twenty-plus years, Rio had avoided anything to do with Christmas. Now, he wore a Santa hat he'd purchased with his own money to replace the one he'd tossed in the trash. And he was serving Christmas punch to a group of homeless veterans, many of them also wearing Santa hats.

If that wasn't enough to make him question his sanity, he'd earlier provided rides for a number of homeless men and women to a shelter for showers and the first of several other gifts awaiting them under the tree. A complete set of clothes, including shoes and socks. Somehow the amazing little joy warrior had learned the sizes of every invited person and purchased accordingly, with steep discounts from local businesses.

"This," she declared as she slowed on a pass of the punch table, "is the real Christmas. Doing the work of Jesus, loving on people in His name. This makes me so, so happy."

He wanted to grab her and kiss her dimpled smile. "I'm not supposed to like Christmas."

"But you do."

He offered a mock scowl. "It's all about commercialism and greed."

"But it's not. Not today anyway. And you know it." Face alight, she said, "I'm so happy you're here."

"Me, too." He saluted her with a punch dipper. "I like watching you work the room. My brothers-in-arms adore you."

She sparkled. He wondered if she had any idea how much he enjoyed observing her zest for life and people.

"They love Brinkley," she said. "He's the star."

Sure enough, the pup moved quietly around the tables, pausing for pets or to be held in someone's lap for a while.

"The food's not bad either." Rio motioned to the buffet tables lined around the edge of the hall. They were loaded with healthy appetizers, fancy charcuterie boards, fruits, cheeses, dips and crackers, and more. "I'm impressed at the way you pulled all this together with limited funds."

"Lots of people helped. Including you. The food was mostly prepared by our volunteers and the center's staff. Wait until you see the cakes the Downtown Bakery donated."

"Speaking of—" He nudged his head toward a set of double doors and two volunteers toting an enormous Christmas cake. Behind them was another that he knew was for the diabetics.

Nobody was forgotten on Eden's watch.

"Ooooh," she squealed in excitement and hurried to the cake table where Taffy snapped photos.

One of the chair-bound veterans waved at Rio.

Rio turned the dipper over to another volunteer and went to the man. "How's it going, Fred?"

"I stayed in my room last year. Thought I'd come this time, seeing as how you're one of us."

"So is Eden. She lost her dad in the Middle East."

"I know it. Shame. He'd sure be proud of her."

"Yes, he would." Rio located the happy elf and wished he was a different kind of man. Becoming a believer didn't change who he was or what he'd done with his life. Or the tasks that still lay before him.

Nothing could change his past, not even God.

"What are you going to do about her, son?" Fred asked.

Rio huffed a half chuckle. "Not sure of your meaning."

The old man cackled. "Yes, you are. I seen you watching her with your heart in your eyes."

Not true. Rio was a better actor than that.

He intentionally hardened his expression. "She does good work for our guys. That's it."

The old man laughed again and Rio turned the topic to the cake. Green frosting created pine branches that dangled ornaments in red and gold. Beneath were insignias representing every branch of service, similar to the baubles on the tree. Written in the center was a poignantly appropriate message for veterans. "Peace on Earth, Good Will to All."

For once, Rio saw the beauty, and even the joy,

in the décor. He'd actually enjoyed assisting Eden and the other volunteers as they'd strung garland and fairy lights and added snow-flocked pine cone centerpieces to the red-and-green-covered tables. Now that the candles and fairy lights were lit, the formerly austere space glowed with festive cheer.

Conversations, also cheerful, hummed over the soft sounds of vintage Christmas carols from Eden's old boom box. She made these men and women happy. She made them feel special, important.

Remembered.

His chest pinched.

He hoped when his time came, someone like Eden was around to remember him, the veteran with no family to care if he lived or died.

The maudlin thought snuck up on him. He forced his focus to his favorite Santa's helper.

Today was a good day. Thanks to her.

Unable to stay away and with no reason to try, Rio joined Eden to carry Christmassy plates of cake to eager recipients. He stopped frequently to share a laugh, a story, or to listen to comments.

Respect was too small a term for these men and women. He was in a room filled with valor. These vets had chosen to do the right thing no matter the personal cost. They represented everything he still fought for.

When the last vet was served, Eden handed him a plate. "Sit and eat with Grandpa, will you please? I'm too busy."

"Sure." Although he'd noticed Steven wasn't alone, he took the cake and a few appetizers to the old cop's table. The leg could use a rest. "Mind if I join you?"

"Have a seat."

He settled in, listened to the men talk and spoke little. He learned more with his mouth closed than opened. Most of the men at this specific table were homeless. Like Eden, her grandpa had sought them out to make them feel welcome. Rio could do no less.

When conversation lulled, he asked each one where and when they'd served. This started a round of stories and more listening on his part.

"Ho-ho-ho! Merry Christmas!"

Rio and others turned toward the sound. Someone dressed as Santa Claus *ho-ho-hoed* his way into the space.

Watching the vets' reactions was priceless. Laughter, nostalgia, pure joy.

"Looky there," one vet hollered. "Old Saint Nick."

Eden's voice rose over the chatter. "Everyone, Santa is here and he has gifts for all of you."

Santa and his helpers began handing out gaily-wrapped gifts.

A single shiny red package in hand, Eden came toward Rio's table.

Her eyes found his. "Thank you for your service, Chief Warrant Officer Hendrix."

Then she wrecked him with a flash of dimples and a gift with his name on it.

"But I didn't expect—" he started, struggling not to overreact. He didn't do Christmas presents. Didn't deserve them.

"I know. Surprising you makes it more special."

The more special part was her. Eden. The bright light who'd stolen his senses.

Looking from her to the gift, Rio thought his chest might break open with emotion.

Later that evening, after the party and cleanup ended, Eden finished loading her car just as Rio and the Homeless Alliance volunteers returned from delivering the homeless veterans to a shelter. Every veteran had left with gifts, food and information about a variety of free or inexpensive services, including lodging.

They'd also listened to Santa read the real Christmas story from the second chapter of Luke before singing "Silent Night" together with a group of caroling children. All in all, the day had gone exactly as she'd dreamed.

"As per your orders, General," Rio said with twinkling eyes as he exited the Mustang. "All military personnel relocated and accounted for."

Brinkley trotted over to escort his new hero to her side. Rio's limp was more pronounced. He'd been on his feet too much today. Brinkley, of course, had noticed.

"Mission accomplished," she responded, "and no one was injured during Operation Veterans Christmas."

"Only our bellies." Rio patted his flat stomach before dropping a casual arm over her shoulders. "You are astounding."

She bumped his side with hers. "Is that a good thing?"

"The best." Growing serious, Rio turned her to face him. "Thank you."

She placed a hand over his heart, felt it thud even as her own heart thudded in response. "My immense pleasure. I loved having you here. You must know that by now." The beat in her chest quickened, but today had been so beautiful, she couldn't stop the flow of words. "I'm falling in love with you, Rio."

"I know." With a heavy sigh, as if she'd just announced a death in the family, he rested his forehead against hers. "I feel the same. If things were different…"

"They could be." She bracketed his face with her hands. "Couldn't they? If we care for each other?"

A dozen emotions flickered through his usually secretive eyes. He stroked his fingertips down her cheek and across her mouth. Her lips parted.

Just as he leaned in to kiss her, his cell phone sounded.

With a wry tilt of his head, he stepped away to answer.

Disappointment crowded in. Eden pushed back. Today was a joy day. Rio cared for her. Even if that's all she'd ever have, she wouldn't complain. He'd told her from the beginning of his intention to get back to his other life. He was not the settling kind.

Though not intending to eavesdrop, she couldn't help overhearing his end of the phone call.

As was often the case, Rio's side of the conversation didn't tell her much. "Yes, sir... I understand, sir... I'll be waiting for your call... Yes, sir. Always."

He hung up and turned back toward her. "That was my boss."

"On a Saturday?"

"Protecting the peace never rests, Eden. Not for guys like me."

"Was it good news or bad?"

He didn't look unhappy. But he didn't look relieved either. "I'll know for sure after a final meeting next week."

A smidgen of Eden's joy seeped out.

So, regardless of her declaration, he still hoped to go back to his career. From what he'd told her, he could be sent anywhere in the world. At any time.

And wherever he went, he traveled alone.

Settling down in a small town was not in his plans.

Chapter Sixteen

Life, he'd learned the hard way, did not go as planned. If it did, Rio would have left Rosemary Ridge the day after JP's wedding. Instead, he'd stayed too long.

Or perhaps not long enough.

Either way, he'd made a crucial error. He'd forgotten to guard his heart.

Nevertheless, he could not regret his newfound faith, the unexpected pleasure of the holidays, or the sweetness of Eden.

"Memories," he muttered to the mirror on Monday morning as he trimmed his beard. Memories he could take with him. But he could not take the person who'd made all those memories possible. Eden.

At 0800 hours, the second call came from headquarters. In no-nonsense terms, Rio learned his fate.

The leak had been discovered. Rio would not be privy to the culprit's identity, but he was cleared of any wrongdoing in the security breach. Although relieved by the outcome, he was not as jubilant as he'd expected to be.

And he knew why.

"Report for assignment tomorrow."

"Tomorrow?" he responded. "Tomorrow's Christmas Eve. Can't this wait until the twenty-sixth?"

A telling silence followed his unusual declaration. He'd never asked for holiday leave.

"Emergencies don't wait."

"Yes, sir. I understand." Duty. Honor. Do the hard things that others couldn't or wouldn't.

But his heart sank to the toes of his awkward boot cast. He'd hoped to spend Christmas Day with Eden. One more good memory to take with him.

"However, this isn't an emergency," the voice on the other end said. "Be here on the twenty-sixth."

A smile rose from Rio's chest to his lips. "Thank you, sir. I'll be there."

"See you then. And, Hendrix? Merry Christmas."

"Merry Christmas, sir."

Merry Christmas. He'd repeated the greeting numerous times this week. Somehow, saying the words, thinking of Christ's birth, the veterans' party, Eden's luminescence, took a little of the edge off that other Christmas, the horrific Christmas when he was twelve.

As the call ended, Rio stared out the hotel window at the inflatables, pondering the news, examining his response. Frosty the Snowman was melting again.

Three more days. Difficult, but for the best. The sooner he made the break, the easier it would be for everyone.

***

On Christmas Eve, Eden closed the salon at three o'clock. Today was the day she delivered Grandpa's pumpkin bread to friends and neighbors, especially the shut-ins or those without family.

She'd invited Rio along for the fun but he'd had errands to run. So far, he'd said nothing more about returning to his job, and Eden hoped he didn't hear anything until after the holidays.

Selfish of her, yes, but for Rio, too. He needed to experience every single minute of a true, Christ-centered Christmas.

"I'll be back in time to change for tonight's candlelight service," she told Grandpa as they boxed up foil-covered tins of pumpkin bread.

"I'll be ready. Is Rio going with us?"

"He's meeting us there." She grinned across the filled boxes. "He said he'd report for church at 1900 hours."

Grandpa coughed a laugh.

Over her protests, he hoisted a box and led the way to the SUV. Brinkley, decked in Santa hat and red bandana, leaped into the passenger seat, ever eager to love on people.

Once everything was loaded, Eden drove around, spreading cheer and pumpkin bread until she ran out.

Shortly before seven, she and Grandpa arrived at the church. Rio met them on the steps. He looked serious, but then he usually did. He also looked handsome enough to be on a magazine cover.

Pressed slacks, gleaming black shoes, maroon shirt and a gray blazer looked incredible on him. And he smelled great, too.

Eden was glad she'd worn the Christmas red dress again.

"Where's the boot?"

"Taking a well-earned break. I'm good. And you look pretty," he said as they made their way into the church, his fingertips at her back. She loved that tiny, protective touch.

"Thank you." Entering the row first, she took a seat. Grandpa stood back, letting Rio sit next to her. "Have you ever attended a candlelight service before?"

"None that I appreciated."

She squeezed his arm. "Things are different now. *You're* different. Did you hear from your boss yet?"

Taking her hand, Rio pulled it close. The pianist began to play "Away in a Manger."

"They're ready to begin. Let's talk after, okay?"

"Okay."

Though his expression revealed nothing, Eden's stomach dipped low.

She spent the rest of the beautiful service in fervent prayer.

"Ride with me?" Rio asked as they departed the church.

"Go ahead, sis. I'll drive your car home," Grandpa said.

Eden kissed her grandfather's cheek and handed

him the keys. "We won't be late. Mom is expecting me to pick her up early tomorrow."

Hopefully, Mom remembered that they'd planned to spend Christmas Day together.

Grandpa waved over one shoulder as he walked away.

Cast in golden shadows, Rio led them along the luminaria-lit sidewalk to his car.

"Nice touch," he said.

"Aren't they? Someone sets them up while we're inside. Even though the church has done them for several years, they're always a surprise. At least to me. The perfect ending to the service."

While the worship team softly played "Oh, Little Town of Bethlehem," a holy hush had shimmered on the gathered faithful. The sanctuary lights had gone down as they'd passed the candlelight from person to person, symbolic of sharing the good news of Jesus's birth.

"Did you enjoy it?" she asked.

"I did." They reached the Mustang. Rio clicked the locks and they got inside.

When he started the engine, the radio came on. They exchanged amused glances as "Have Yourself a Merry Little Christmas" oozed from the speakers.

"You caught me," he said and drove out of the church parking lot. The glow of candlelight in paper bags faded, but not the glow in Eden's spirit.

"That makes me happy."

"Is there anything that doesn't make you happy?"

"Yes." Amusement seeped away. "You leaving."

She angled her knees toward him. "Isn't that what we need to talk about?"

"I got the call from headquarters yesterday." He circled the Mustang around the block and headed toward her neighborhood. "The job issues have resolved. My top-security clearances remain intact. I'm needed back at work."

She swallowed a cry of protest and forced a tremulous smile. "Congratulations. This is what you wanted, wasn't it?"

He hesitated and Eden wondered what was going on inside his head.

Finally, he said, "I'm grateful for a second chance to do the only thing I know, to use my skills for the greater good. My career is my life, my purpose. I made that choice a long time ago, Eden."

Eden wanted to argue but she heard the decision in his voice. She was not important enough to change his mind.

"When?" She fought against the ache in her voice. The one that matched her heart.

"The day after Christmas. JP and Zoey invited me for Christmas dinner tomorrow. Can't pass up her pecan pie."

"Will you have breakfast with us then? Grandpa is making his should-be-famous French toast."

Rio stopped in front of her house and put the car in Park but left the engine running. Like him, running to somewhere else, somewhere he either would not—or could not—ask her to go.

Not that she could go with him anyway. Her life

was here, caring for Mom and Grandpa. Rio didn't need her. Her family did.

"If you still want me," he replied, "I'd love to come for breakfast."

Oh, she wanted him, all right. "I'm bringing Mom from Golden Leaves for the day. Are you okay with meeting her? We never know how clear she'll be or if she'll get confused or upset. Sometimes she's angry or belligerent."

Rio touched her hand. Kind, gentle, tender. "I'd be honored to meet her. Regardless."

"Okay, then." Eden grappled for the door handle, needing to escape before she embarrassed herself by crying. "Thanks for the ride."

"Eden—"

Before he could stop her, or play the gentleman, Eden hopped out of the car.

"Good night. See you in the morning."

She slammed the door and hurried up the walkway.

Rio slept soundly that night. Decision made. Time to move forward.

Eden had taken the news of his imminent departure fairly well, he thought, all things considered. Even though they'd been acquainted years ago, this time had been different. They'd become more than friends. Parting could have been sticky.

Rio didn't like sticky relationships.

But he sure liked her.

The promised Christmas morning with her family wasn't as awkward as he'd expected. Although there were only four of them, conversation flowed with ease to the backdrop of Eden's endless Christmas music, Brinkley's antics and Steven's delicious French toast and hot spiced cider.

Rio felt almost at home, a bizarre emotion for a nomad, as if Christmas had been waiting for him right there under an evergreen tree along with the small crèche of Baby Jesus.

A pleasant experience for a change. But he was who he was. Duty and honor called.

He needed to keep reminding himself of that.

After breakfast, they gathered in the living room where Steven read the Christmas story from the Bible and spoke briefly about that miraculous morning that changed the world.

Though the story was ages old and he'd heard it at the party and again last night at church, this year the verses from Luke sounded new and real. Real, in a way they never had before.

His father had been wrong, terribly wrong. In more ways than one.

As Steven closed the well-worn black Bible, Eden's mother burst out in song.

For a surprised moment, she sang "Joy to the World" alone, her voice clear and pure, her face shining.

Then Eden slid an arm over her mother's shoulders and joined in. Steven followed suit in a raspy, breathy baritone for a few words here and there.

Touched, Rio could do no less than join them.

Even he knew the first verse to such a famous carol. To "Silent Night," as well, the next song in Mrs. Carnegie's repertoire. Even though her memory was fading, dementia could not steal the deep-seated music.

When the sing-along ended, the Christmas elf, her reindeer ears jiggling atop her head, began passing gifts from beneath the tree.

Rio patted himself on the back for his last-minute shopping trips. Gloves for Steven and warm scarves for Eden and her mother, the latter a purchase he'd driven an hour last night to find and was grateful for the few shops still open on Christmas Eve.

Eden's mother—a pretty woman with her daughter's soft brown eyes—received his present with a pleased smile.

"Do I know you?" she asked.

Gently, he answered, "I'm Rio Hendrix, ma'am. Eden's friend."

"Oh, yes." But she clearly could not place him, although Eden had introduced him more than once already this morning.

Slowly, with painstaking care, she unwrapped the present, removed the soft scarf and pressed it against her cheek, eyes closed, and smile vague, as if lost in a different memory.

He ached for the woman and the road both she and her family were walking. Brave, brave family. Warriors doing the right thing, no matter the personal cost.

No wonder he'd fallen for Eden. Although their

battlegrounds differed, they shared a moral compass to fight for others and to do what was right regardless of the cost to themselves.

Steven broke the lull by tearing into his present with glee.

"Real leather," he exclaimed. "I need these."

He slid the gloves onto his hands and kept them on even as he opened the other gifts Eden piled next to his chair.

Unexpected heat warmed Rio's chest. He was no stranger to gift giving, but most of his past gifts had had strings attached. These did not.

Eden sat cross-legged under the tree to open her gifts. She chose his first.

A small tension rose in Rio. He wanted to make her happy, especially today.

"Puppies!" Eden squealed as she swirled the dog-printed scarf around her neck. "I love it, Rio. Real cashmere. It's so soft. I'll think of you every time I wear it."

He smiled at her childlike enthusiasm, her joy, though he'd expected no less from Miss Optimism. Today was Christmas, the day to celebrate Jesus, her favorite holiday. If she was sad, she refused to show it.

He was not the right man for her, and her actions today proved that she knew this truth. She'd soldier on without him, find someone else, as she should. He wanted that for her, yet he struggled to think of *his* Eden with another man.

He prayed—yes, he did—that nothing he did or

said would leave a wound or darken the light shining from her.

"Now, open yours." Eden indicated the two packages he held on his lap. "One from Grandpa and one from me."

"You didn't need to buy me anything."

"Your first Christmas as a believer? Oh, yes we did."

Rio opened Steven's gift first, saving Eden's for the last.

"A man can always use a good survival knife," Steven said. "Eden got me a similar one years ago."

The rosewood handle was engraved with a Bible verse. *The Lord is my strength and my shield.*

The verse felt especially fitting. He'd always operated in his own strength and protection. Now, he had something—Someone—far better on his side.

"Thanks, Steven." His chest was getting clogged with unfamiliar emotion. And he still had to open Eden's gift.

Setting the new knife aside, Rio slowly unwrapped the rectangular package. Inside was a men's handsome devotional Bible.

"That's Grandpa's favorite." Eden's expression was alive with hope. "I know you like to read so…"

Rio ran a palm over the smooth leather and his name engraved in one corner, a lump in his throat. "I'll read this every day. It's beautiful."

She was beautiful.

The atmospheric emotion was about to choke him. In an effort to regain his composure, Rio left the gifts on the chair and began to collect the discarded wrapping paper. Brinkley grabbed scattered paper and trotted away with it.

"Hey!"

A laughing, dimpled Eden, trash bag in hand, waved him off. "Shredding paper is his idea of Christmas." In a low tone, she added, "Mom's having a good day, and she's thrilled with the scarf. Look at her touching it."

Sure enough, the older woman rubbed the soft material against her cheek even while she and Steven chatted about their favorite Christmas memories.

Paper crinkled as Eden shoved trash into the bag. "When did you have the opportunity to shop?"

"Yours, I've had awhile. The others, last night." Bending low, he raked a pile of discarded ribbon from under a chair.

"After you dropped me off?"

"Yep." Finding an open store had been a challenge, and he'd driven the extra miles. For her. To soften tomorrow's departure. Maybe for both of them.

With a tender look that turned her brown eyes soft and shiny, Eden placed a hand on his arm. "You are a kind and thoughtful soul."

Fighting emotion, he intentionally scowled.

If she knew how unkind he could be, even for a worthy cause, she wouldn't say such things. He was glad she didn't know. "Don't blow my cover."

He meant it, but her reaction showed just how little she understood who he was.

With a laugh, she stuck a discarded bow on his shoulder and kissed his cheek.

Eden messed with his head, his determination, his reasoning.

Leaving was imperative before he did something stupid. Like stay and ruin her life.

Dinner that night with JP and Zoey at the House of Hope was the polar opposite of breakfast with Eden. Noisy versus quiet. Chaos versus calm. And enough food to feed four teenagers, two toddlers and seven adults, including him, Brandt's fiancée and a homeless couple Zoey had befriended.

To his dismay, his two old buddies had purchased gifts for him. "My apologies for not bringing anything for you."

"You're here. That's our present this year," JP said.

"About that." He pushed his plate away, having eaten more today than was prudent. Two pieces of pie might have been pushing it. A man didn't get homemade pecan pie in the places he lived. "I'm leaving tomorrow."

The table quieted as the announcement sank in.

Brandt put down his coffee cup. "Is your leg healed enough for the long ride?"

He'd ridden his Harley a few times since graduating to only the boot, but with orders to report tomorrow, he'd have to ship the bike. "I'm flying out."

"What about Eden?" This from Zoey. "I thought…" She let the rest drift away.

"Nice woman." He winked, tried to joke. "Too nice for me."

With a scowl on his face, JP scraped his chair away from the table and pointed at Rio. "You, me, Brandt. Rec room now. Let's talk."

"Nothing to talk about." But he and Brandt followed JP to the privacy of a room with a pool table and big-screen TV. A problem-solving room for the foster boys, JP had once told him. Conversation was easier if their hands were busy.

"Chalk up." JP offered each man a pool cue. "And start talking."

"I only came to town for your wedding." Rio took the cue stick, leaving out the rest of his agenda. His dad. The reinstatement from Uncle Sam.

"Nice, but things change."

"They haven't."

"If you say you don't have feelings for Eden Carnegie, I'll call you a liar to your face. We've noticed."

"I might have to punch you," Rio replied, slow and easy, not really meaning the threat.

JP shrugged. "You have before. I can handle your wimpy punches. What I can't handle is you leaving this town with regrets."

"I live my life without regrets, JP, which is part of the reason I won't subject Eden to who I am. I'm a loner. A misfit who found his purpose as an intelligence operative doing the dirty work no one else can or will do. I don't fit in civilian life." He chalked up his cue.

"Seems to me—" Brandt took the blue chalk square from him "—you've been fitting in real fine. Fundraisers, Christmas parties, church, and lot of hours in the company of a pretty dog groomer who shines when you're around."

"She deserves better than me." With a vicious slam of cue against ball, he took his shot. Balls scattered, clattering, like his thoughts and his heart.

His pals were messing with his head and, thanks to this morning with Eden and her family, he was already having enough trouble in that direction.

"My mind is made up." He jabbed the three ball toward the side pocket and missed.

Brandt elbowed him out of the way. "John-Parker and I've talked about this. Why not join Silent Security? Our business is growing faster than we can hire experienced people we trust. With your skill set, you'd be invaluable."

"You trust me? After all these years?"

JP pressed the cue stick against his chest. "With our lives. Like always. Brothers can be apart, but they're still brothers."

The hard lump in Rio's chest grew larger. These guys were his brothers, even now.

His own blood kin wouldn't speak to him, but these two men—and Eden—wanted him in their lives.

"The offer means more than I can say, but I can't stay."

"So you're telling us you don't care about Eden Carnegie?"

Staring down at the scatter of striped and solid balls, Rio finally admitted the truth. "I care too much."

Far too much. He loved her. And if he loved her, he'd get out of her life before her light dimmed and she lost her joy.

No matter what they said, or in spite of the gratifying job offer, Rio knew what he had to do. Eden deserved the best. And that was not him.

Chapter Seventeen

He shouldn't have done it.

Rio had mentally promised not to see Eden again before leaving for the Tulsa airport.

Yet, bright and early the next morning, he'd stood, poinsettia in hand, on her front porch.

Refusing to go inside, he'd said goodbye, kissed her cheek, and driven away without making promises he couldn't keep. No promise to call or write or email. No promise to someday return to Rosemary Ridge. Make the break and move on.

Depending on where Uncle Sam sent him, he might not be able to contact her anyway. Too dangerous. Too much opportunity to be intercepted by the wrong people. He wouldn't take the chance of putting her or himself in danger.

But as Rio found his seat number on the airplane and stashed his bag in the overhead compartment, he couldn't get Eden's face out of his mind.

She'd smiled and wished him well, but her eyes had told a different story.

He'd never forget those beautiful, soft, caring eyes. Or her dimpled smile. And he'd always treasure the tender, accepting way she'd listened the night he'd dumped his ugly past in her lap. He'd felt loved.

For a short time, her light had shined on him, and he was a better man because of her.

When he'd said his goodbyes, Eden had touched his cheek and promised to pray for him. Every single day. Forever.

Now, on the plane, he tilted his head back against the seat and prayed for her in return. That he hadn't caused her too much grief, that she'd never lose her glow. He even asked God to send her the kind of love she wanted and deserved.

As the plane lifted off, normally his favorite part of the flight, he opened his cell phone and scrolled through the photos. Eden grooming dogs, laughing. Always smiling. Eden at the veterans' home, the party, Christmas morning. Eden at JP's wedding, heart-stoppingly beautiful. Eden in a Santa hat, eyes wide with delight, at the fundraiser. Over ice cream.

When had he ever snapped so many pictures of anyone? Pictures he couldn't take with him on assignment for safety reasons. But the thought of deleting them filled him with grief.

Pictures were all he'd have left of her.

The woman seated next to him glanced over. "Pretty lady. Your wife?"

"A friend." He scrolled to a photo of Eden and him slow dancing at JP's wedding. Taffy had sent it to him.

"A very good friend, it appears," the woman said.

"Yes." Rio put the phone away and turned to stare out the window. He didn't feel up to conversation with a chatty seatmate.

JP and Brandt had urged him to pray about his decision. And they'd told him to listen to God's leading. He wasn't sure how that worked, but the pressure in his chest needed release.

Closing his eyes against the stretchy white clouds drifting by the plane, Rio let the past few weeks roll through his thoughts as he again mentally talked to a Savior he'd only just begun to believe in.

He'd come to Rosemary Ridge to attend a wedding and to see his father. Though not unexpectedly, he'd failed at the latter. He had not, however, planned on falling in love or questioning everything in his life.

Nor had he planned on a broken bone or a sparkling Jesus follower with her pack of dogs.

From the time he was twelve, Rio had felt different, alone, including the years with Miss Mamie, JP and Brandt. Even then, he'd kept that awful part of his past hidden.

Until now, he'd never felt lonely.

Today, he did. A yearning as strong as the pull to do the right thing, the hard thing, to follow the moral code he lived by.

A hollow homesickness expanded in his belly.

The man without a home wanted to go home. To the only place he'd felt loved since his mother's death. To Eden.

"God, help me to know Your will," he whispered, and pressed his forehead hard against the cool window, hoping he hadn't lost his mind completely. And hoping even more that God would hear and answer.

Eden's cell phone chirped for the eighth time that morning. Though she'd stopped hoping it was Rio after the fourth text from Taffy and Zoey, her pulse still sped up.

"He's gone, Brinkley." She turned off the hair dryer and spoke to the forlorn dog staring at her over the end of his sleigh bed. "And rightly so. He's trying to save the world, which is far more important than we are."

The other dogs in the salon seemed unusually quiet this morning, too. Like Brinkley, they read her mood even as she tried to remain positive.

Taking the cell phone from the counter, she texted back without reading the message.

I'm fine. Thanks. Talk later. Busy now. Got a stray to clean up.

She returned to the large, mixed-breed dog, feeling sorry for any animal that had spent the holiday scavenging in the trash. The scrawny dog was fortunate Grandpa had caught her digging in theirs.

"We'll get you prettied up and find you a home," Eden said. She was unsure of the breeds involved, but probably a spaniel and Labrador due to the furry long ears, golden color and sweet nature.

Carefully detangling the matted ears, Eden's heart jumped when the doorknob to her salon turned. She tamped it down. Probably Grandpa again. After spending most of the morning with her in the salon, he'd walked over twice already this afternoon.

She couldn't hide her disappointment from him, even though she'd tried. His words of sound biblical advice had comforted her, including a truth she'd experienced before. A broken heart would take time to heal, but God was still good and He had an even better plan for her life.

"I love you, Grandpa," she said, turning toward the door to reassure him again that she was okay. "I'm fi—"

Her heart stopped, stuttered, started again.

"Rio?"

Brinkley leaped from his bed and raced to the entry, jumping and barking.

The stray on her grooming table joined in with a few yips of her own as Rio stepped into the room, larger than life and ten times more wonderful.

"I like your pretty words, but I'm not Grandpa."

No, he certainly was not.

Eden's brain started to spin. The grooming brush in her hand clattered to floor. "What? How? I don't understand."

"Neither do I. Not completely. On the first flight, I prayed, and I realized some things."

"Such as?"

He crouched to rub Brinkley's overexcited head.

"This may be my only opportunity to gain some of the things missing in my life. Things I want but can never have in my line of work."

"What kinds of things?"

"A home, real friends I trust." He locked eyes with her. "And if I'm very fortunate, a good woman to love."

Was he saying what she thought he was saying?

"What about your career? You do important work. You make the world safer."

One of his blacker-than-night eyebrows lifted. "Do you want me to go?"

"No! But this is not about me. I want you do what's right for you." No matter how much losing him hurt.

"At some point, every man in the spy game either retires or gets killed."

A spy. The idea had seemed preposterous. Until now.

"I can't bear if you get killed."

Humor sparked in his eyes. "Not too fond of the idea myself. Retirement sounds less painful."

"Retirement?" Eden's heart jumped into her throat. "Are you really thinking of retiring?"

"I don't know if I can fit into this thing called civilian life, but I'd like to try. JP and Brandt think I can. What do you think?"

Mind racing, pulse banging in her temple, Eden unleashed the stray and let her hop to the floor.

"With God's help, you can do anything you set your mind to, Rio."

"There's something strong between us, something real and special," he said. "I realize it's happened fast, so I'll give you all the time you need, but on that plane ride, thinking I'd never see you again made me face the truth. I don't deserve you, but I need you, and I'm in love with you. I'll do everything in my power to earn your love in return."

The happiness in Eden's chest bloomed onto her face.

Rio was back. He loved her enough to return.

"You can't earn my love, Rio," she said and then seeing his frown, hurried to finish. "Love is a gift. And I give it freely. To you, the generous, caring, valiant, complicated warrior I've prayed for God to send my way."

"So, you're willing to see where the future takes us, even knowing there are things I can never share with you, secrets I'll take to the grave?" His shoulders tensed.

"You are the sum of all your experiences with a happy dose of Jesus to lighten you up. You are who you are, and I love that man."

With a relieved sigh, Rio opened his arms and Eden walked in.

Placing her cheek over his heart, she relished the strength and tenderness of his embrace, and thanked God for a second chance to love and be loved by the right man. Her sensitive, mysterious warrior. Rio Hendrix.

Epilogue

New Year's Day was generally quiet at Eden's house. With traditional Southern ham, black-eyed peas and cornbread on the stove, she, Grandpa and Mom always watched the Rose Parade. But this year Rio joined her on the couch, one arm slung over her shoulders as if he loved touching her—which she knew he did.

Since the day after Christmas, they'd spent every day together, including New Year's Eve. He'd accompanied her to the veterans' center for the afternoon and then taken her to an elegant dinner in a rotating restaurant atop a hotel.

She was still reliving the midnight kiss as they'd stood at the sky-high windows overlooking the city lights.

Leaning her head against his shoulder, Eden grew more confident every day of their future together. Rio had taken a job with his foster brothers' security business and was looking for a house to buy.

The nomad wanted to put down roots.

Grandpa's landline jangled above the sounds of a marching band.

Her grandpa held up a palm when she started to rise. "I've got this."

She settled again, praying this was the surprise Grandpa had been working on.

In seconds, her thoughts were confirmed.

Grandpa held out the receiver. "Rio. For you."

"Me?" Rio unwound his arm from the pleasant comfort of Eden's shoulder and stood. "Who is it?"

The only people he could think of who might call him here were JP or Brandt. Did he have a security assignment already?

"You'll see."

Puzzled by the older man's cryptic smile and mysterious manner, Rio took the receiver. "Hello?"

"Rio Hendrix?"

"Who's calling?"

"Isaac Swadley."

Instantly, Rio recognized the name. The prison warden.

"Is everything all right?" He didn't dare hope this was good news.

"Fine. I have a message for you." Was that a smile in the serious warden's voice?

"A message? From my dad?" Rio's voice cracked on the end.

"He'd like to speak with you. Hold on. You have five minutes."

Rio had never fainted in his life but all the blood drained from his brain. Dots danced before his eyes. He leaned against the nearest wall, listening to the crackling movement noises on the other end of the phone.

A different voice came on the line. "Rio?"

"Dad?"

"It's me, son."

Son. Carlton Hendrix, the man who'd rejected him for twenty-plus years, had called him *son*.

For the allotted five minutes, Rio mostly listened, his pulse banging against his temple, his throat tight with shock and disbelief.

When the call ended, he remained where he was for several seconds, contemplating what had just happened.

Eden came to stand next to him, her hand against his back. "Are you okay?"

"That was my dad. He said I was right. And that he was sorry. For everything." Except for the voice, the prisoner Hendrix had sounded nothing like the harsh, controlling know-it-all Rio recalled. The man had sounded old and broken.

"Oh, Rio, that's wonderful news."

He ran a hand over his face to wipe away the shock as reality sat in. After more than twenty years his dad had not only agreed to talk, he'd admitted that he deserved to be in prison. That he'd failed as a husband, a father and as a human being.

"How did this happen?" he asked. "Did you have something to do with this? Is this why the warden called here?"

Eden pointed toward the living room where Steven appeared focused on the parade and a troupe of

Irish dancers. "Grandpa knows the warden. They were in the academy together."

"You told Steven?"

"Grandpa already knew about your dad. I only confirmed that he'd blamed you and refused communications...and that his behavior hurt you. Please don't be upset that I told."

"Upset?" He pointed at the phone. "I'm grateful. To you and Steven both. And to the warden. I don't know how he did it but—"

"I know how he did it. Grandpa went to the prison and spoke to your dad."

"He did that for me?"

Steven's voice came from the living room. "She went, too."

Rio turned incredulous gaze on her beautiful, smiling face. "You did? You saw my dad?"

Eden nodded. "I wanted him to know about the incredible son he had, about your service to this country and all the good you'd done in this world, all the sacrifices you've made for others. I wanted him to know that he should be proud of you. And before we left, he let us pray for him. Isn't that wonderful?"

She melted him. There was no longer any doubt in Rio's mind that Eden loved him with a real and lasting love. She knew his most painful secret and still she'd gone into a dark, scary place to fight for him when he couldn't.

"I don't even know what to say except that I love you more than I thought I could love anyone. Getting run over by your pack of dogs is the best thing that ever happened to me."

Eden dimpled. "All things worked out for our good."

She was right about that as well.

He bent to kiss her sweet mouth before admitting, "I have a surprise for you, too. I was saving it for later when we're alone, but now seems a good time."

"I love surprises."

"Two, actually. I hope you like them."

"Tell me. What's the first?"

"Sadie."

"The stray dog I'm trying to find a home for?"

"I found her one. With me."

"Oh, I could just kiss you." And she did. "What's the second surprise?"

"Promise to kiss me for this one, too?"

She gave him a saucy toss of her head. "If I like your surprise."

"Come outside with me."

"Do I need my coat?"

Rio winked. "I'll keep you warm."

"Sounds good to me." She followed him outside to his Harley.

Opening his saddlebag, he extracted a thick envelope and handed it to her. "Open it."

Curious, Eden removed the paperwork and read. "Is this a contract for a house?"

"I haven't signed it yet, but they accepted my offer for the house on Mockingbird Lane."

"The one with the gorgeous kitchen and huge

backyard?" She pressed the papers to her heart. "I love that house."

"If I buy it, will you live it in with me? As my wife?"

Instead of a reply, she pulled his head down and kissed him, long and deep, and with enough heart that he knew the answer was yes. This amazing woman would be his wife, share his life, his home and, hopefully, the children they both wanted.

When the joyous kissing ended, he refused to let her go and she snuggled close to his chest.

"I take it," he said with a smile in his voice, "that you like my second surprise?"

"Yes, oh, yes," she said, laughing up at him. "I like it very much. And I love you even more."

With a sigh, he rocked her close and offered thanks to the God he wasn't supposed to believe in.

He'd come back to Rosemary Ridge never expecting to find everything that he hadn't known was missing in his life.

Faith. Love. A home. And a hope for a future he'd never thought possible.

Right here in Rosemary Ridge. He'd begun his visit with a broken leg and ended up with a mended heart—and soul.

Miss Mamie would be so pleased to know her rebellious "street rat" had finally come home to stay.

And Rio was pretty happy about it himself.

* * * * *

Dear Reader,

I hope you've enjoyed *His Christmas Journey Home*, the final book in the House of Hope series. (If you haven't read the others, they are still available!) The idea for a series about three boys, now men, raised in the same foster home, first came to me years ago. But, like most of my stories, they needed time to grow in my subconscious until one day all three men suddenly appeared in my head. I intentionally saved Rio's story for last because he was the "brother" who, despite his exceptional intellect and abilities, seemed the most lost. Because of his Scrooge-like cynicism, I couldn't resist pairing him with Eden, the most caring, optimist, Christmas-loving dog groomer in Rosemary Ridge. The addition of adorable dogs and some crusty veterans was, as they say, icing on the cake—the Christmas cake!

For over twenty years, I've been privileged to share my stories with you, and during this holiday season, I want to say a special thank you to all who buy my books, connect on social media, or join my newsletter at www.lindagoodnight.com. You've made my dreams come true. May you feel the holy joy of Christmas this year as never before.

Merry Christmas and Happy Holidays!
Linda Goodnight

Get up to 4 Free Books!

We'll send you 2 free books from each series you try PLUS a free Mystery Gift.

Both the **Love Inspired**® and **Love Inspired**® Suspense series feature compelling novels filled with inspirational romance, faith, forgiveness and hope.

YES! Please send me 2 FREE novels from the Love Inspired or Love Inspired Suspense series and my FREE gift (gift is worth about $10 retail). After receiving them, if I don't wish to receive any more books, I can return the shipping statement marked "cancel." If I don't cancel, I will receive 6 brand-new Love Inspired Larger-Print books or Love Inspired Suspense Larger-Print books every month and be billed just $7.19 each in the U.S. or $7.99 each in Canada. That is a savings of 20% off the cover price. It's quite a bargain! Shipping and handling is just 50¢ per book in the U.S. and $1.25 per book in Canada.* I understand that accepting the 2 free books and gift places me under no obligation to buy anything. I can always return a shipment and cancel at any time by calling the number below. The free books and gift are mine to keep no matter what I decide.

Choose one: ☐ **Love Inspired Larger-Print** (122/322 BPA G36Y)   ☐ **Love Inspired Suspense Larger-Print** (107/307 BPA G36Y)   ☐ **Or Try Both!** (122/322 & 107/307 BPA G36Z)

Name (please print)

Address   Apt. #

City   State/Province   Zip/Postal Code

Email: Please check this box ☐ if you would like to receive newsletters and promotional emails from Harlequin Enterprises ULC and its affiliates. You can unsubscribe anytime.

Mail to the Harlequin Reader Service:
IN U.S.A.: P.O. Box 1341, Buffalo, NY 14240-8531
IN CANADA: P.O. Box 603, Fort Erie, Ontario L2A 5X3

Want to explore our other series or interested in ebooks? Visit www.ReaderService.com or call 1-800-873-8635.

---

*Terms and prices subject to change without notice. Prices do not include sales taxes, which will be charged (if applicable) based on your state or country of residence. Canadian residents will be charged applicable taxes. Offer not valid in Quebec. This offer is limited to one order per household. Books received may not be as shown. Not valid for current subscribers to the Love Inspired or Love Inspired Suspense series. All orders subject to approval. Credit or debit balances in a customer's account(s) may be offset by any other outstanding balance owed by or to the customer. Please allow 4 to 6 weeks for delivery. Offer available while quantities last.

Your Privacy—Your information is being collected by Harlequin Enterprises ULC, operating as Harlequin Reader Service. For a complete summary of the information we collect, how we use this information and to whom it is disclosed, please visit our privacy notice located at https://corporate.harlequin.com/privacy-notice. Notice to California Residents – Under California law, you have specific rights to control and access your data. For more information on these rights and how to exercise them, visit https://corporate.harlequin.com/california-privacy. For additional information for residents of other U.S. states that provide their residents with certain rights with respect to personal data, visit https://corporate.harlequin.com/other-state-residents-privacy-rights/.